A picture tells a tho

"This is great!" Eric cried, grabbing the paper and looking it over with a huge grin. "It's perfect. Don't you think so?"

"Sure," she lied. She didn't know why nothing seemed perfect anymore. Eric, the baseball madness, their lovey-dovey picture in the paper — it was all starting to feel wrong somehow. But the only thing she could pinpoint was that photo. When she'd first looked at it she'd wondered why the caption had read, *Best Couple.* What did that label mean? And who were those people, anyway?

**Other Point paperbacks
you will want to read:**

point

TOTALLY HOT

#1 Losing Control

Linda A. Cooney

SCHOLASTIC INC.
New York Toronto London Auckland Sydney

ISBN 0-590-44560-X

12 11 10 9 8 7 6 5 4 3 2   1 2 3 4 5 6/9

Printed in the U.S.A.   01

First Scholastic printing, August 1991

ONE

Miss Student Activities.

That's what her father called her. One of her teachers had labeled her Miss Perfect, and she'd been called by other names, too. Miss Helper. Miss 4.0. Miss Junior Class.

Miranda Jamison tried not to let the names bother her. So what if she'd headed up last year's Christmas can drive . . . crepe-papered the goalposts . . . got one of the highest scores on the PSATs? Miranda thrived on her meetings, her tutoring, her volunteering, and her grades. She was determined to get the most out of high school, and nothing was going to throw her off course.

Still, every once in a while, just when Miranda's work and planning were at their most intense, she started to feel a little lost. It reminded her of sand slipping away under her feet, when

1

an ocean wave rolled out from the Crescent Bay shore. And while it wasn't a big deal, it left her feeling unsteady, almost wobbly.

But Miranda didn't look unsteady that Thursday afternoon. She was standing in front of the student activities bulletin board. From the toes of her polished riding boots, to the ends of her thick, dark hair, she looked perfectly pulled together. Her red blazer was unwrinkled, even though she'd been through a whole day of classes and after-school meetings as president of the junior class. The shoulder strap of her briefcase rested on her shoulder like it had lived there forever. And yet, there was still something off balance. The feeling, the lost sensation, the sand rushing out from under her feet.

"Just concentrate on something else until Kat gets here," Miranda whispered to herself.

The activities bulletin board was in the hallway just outside the guidance office, and any minute Miranda's best friend, Kat McDonough, would show up to meet her. Then the two of them would walk over to the football field where Miranda's boyfriend, Eric, was finishing his practice.

Miranda pulled her notebook out of her soft leather briefcase, then checked her things-to-do list against the events posted on the activity board.

Things to Do:

Monday — *Student council meeting. Honor Society.*
Tuesday — *Comp due. Dinner out with Dad and*
    Eric.
Wednesday — *Service Club. Beach cleanup meeting.*
Thursday — *Chem quiz. Quad project meeting.*
    (Fix up blind date for Kat.)
Friday — *Volunteer tutoring. International Club.*
    Eric's football game!
    Go to the Wave Cafe with the gang!!!

Besides all her school activities, Miranda also believed in working and planning for her friends. At a moment's notice she was ready to throw a party, help with homework, or loan out her best clothes. And after nights of thinking and worrying, she'd come up with a plan that would put Kat's life back on track.

"Miraaaaaandaaa!"

"Kat?"

"YOOO-HOOOOO!"

Miranda spun around the second she heard Kat's strong voice, which wasn't coming from the quad, but from the direction of the student parking lot. Kat was weaving through the few cars left, hooting like some tropical bird. Kat's short hair was wet, and she was wearing a typical Kat outfit — walking shorts, leather cap, a man's vest, and T-shirt, all of which looked like it had been thrown on her slim swimmer's body in about five seconds. As Kat wove closer, Miranda also saw Kat's famous makeshift necklace. Today her nose plug was hanging from it, along with a pin that read, *Crescent Bay is for Lovers!* with the word *lovers* crossed out and *jokers* written in.

"I thought you were going to stay on campus and rehearse with Gabe at the radio station," Miranda remembered. Kat and their close buddy Gabe Sachs broadcast a popular comedy/talk show over KHOT, the noontime Crescent Bay High radio station.

Kat gave Miranda a big hug. "Gabe was too busy throwing himself at some adoring freshman, so I decided to do a workout over at the public pool. Just because swim team isn't happening now is no reason why I should let my stroke go down the tubes. There's nothing like a little water therapy to get out your frustration." She leaped into a musclewoman pose. "Am I late?"

"Just on time."

"Which means you wanted me to be early."

"*Kat.*"

"Miranda, I've known you since Brownies. I can tell when you're in one of those moods."

"What moods?"

"Those manic, I-have-to-do-everything-right-now, and-if-I-don't-do-it-all-perfectly, I'm-a-total-failure moods."

Miranda had to smile. "I can read your mood today, too."

"Oh, yeah?"

"You're in one of those, somebody's-going-to-laugh-at-me, so-I-guess-I'd-better-make-the-first-joke mood."

Kat grinned. "That strategy has done me a lot of good. I highly recommend it."

"Yeah. I've seen how much good it's done you," Miranda joked back. She put her notebook back in her briefcase and swung the long strap over her shoulder. "We should get going. I told Eric I'd meet him at the field at four-thirty."

Kat held her back and shook her head. "Eric, Eric, Eric. It's good to keep guys waiting, Miranda. It builds character."

"How could you know what's good for

guys?" Miranda bantered as Kat began to tickle her.

"I don't. I just keep my distance, which is so much more fun."

"Yeah. Right." Miranda started tickling back, and pretty soon she was laughing, too. Just seeing Kat's pretty face and witty smile had already made her feel better. They'd been best friends since fifth grade, even though they were as different as two sixteen-year-olds could be. Miranda was leggy and tall and wore tiny diamond earrings her father had given her for her sixteenth birthday, while Kat was blonde and small and dressed like someone's little brother. But the difference went a lot further than looks. Miranda thought things out. Even her relationship with Eric Geraci, captain of the winning football team, had progressed from first date to steady weekends without a hitch or a look back. Meanwhile, Kat was a whirlwind. She'd had a wild romance last summer and not a single date since.

"Is Jojo meeting us, too?" Kat asked, looking around for Joanne Hernandez, the third of their old grade-school trio.

Miranda shook her head. "Jojo has cheerleading practice. And Chip went to that recycling rally." Chip Kohler was Gabe's best friend, another important member of their small, tightly knit group. "We'll all see each other at the game tomorrow night."

"Oh, right." Kat tapped her head to shake water out of her ears. "I still can't believe that Eric's team is undefeated. If we win, the town may just dip Eric in bronze and stick him on the middle of Ocean Avenue. Can you believe that you are dating the captain of an undefeated football team? It's like being Miss America or something."

Miranda got that unsteady feeling again. "Miss America?" *Another name.*

"It's a joke, Miranda."

"I know." Miranda smiled. "Let's go."

"Hold on. You're always in such a hurry. Since I'm here, let me at least check the activity board." Kat stepped up close and squinted at the fliers and the lists. "Hey, look. I didn't know you were picked for that Friends in Need thing."

"What?"

"That peer counseling thing." Kat pointed to the glass-covered board. "Your name is on the list for new counselors."

"Good," Miranda answered in a distracted voice. She was picked for so many things:

Homecoming Princess; Rotary Club speeches; leadership camp. Friends in Need was a peer counseling program where students were trained to talk to other kids who were having a hard time. When the time came for the orientation meeting, she would mark it in her list of things to do. "See anything else important?"

Kat shook her head. "Everything else is for dances, or activities that have romantic possibilities with the opposite sex. That counts me out. Let's go."

Miranda led Kat across the quad, past the library, and toward the main entrance, where a case displayed trophies from the 1920s on. Like the small northern California town of Crescent Bay, their high school was a mixture of charming old and glitzy new. Their cafeteria was overcrowded, but they had a brand-new computer room. Just like the downtown still had a beachfront arcade with a rickety roller coaster, along with the luxurious, newly opened Tucker Resort.

Miranda and Kat trotted down the front steps and around the circular driveway, where buses pulled up in the morning, and past the famous sea lion statue put up by the class of 1948. Miranda thought about the old and the new.

In the old days — the pre-Eric days — Miranda and Kat had been inseparable. But all that had changed last July 4th, when the two of them snuck away from the regulation beach fireworks and went to the amusement park instead.

Miranda's father said the old beachfront amusement park was off limits. But Miranda's lost feeling was strong that night, and it gave her the urge to do something crazy. Kat was always ready to do something crazy, and for once in her life, Miranda gave in, too. She and Kat rode the old roller coaster, and they met two out-of-town guys — Jeff and Grady, from Santa Cruz.

But after a while, Miranda's nerve had fled. Unfortunately Kat wouldn't leave with her. Miranda didn't see her until the next day, and by then Kat was madly, wildly in love. But Grady left town and never called Kat again. Worse, Kat never told Miranda exactly what had happened. For the rest of the summer, Kat cried easily; she moped; she was the one who was lost. By fall her wisecracks had become more pointed, and she'd vowed only to think of guys as friends.

"So did you get down on one knee and ask perfect Eric to the Turnaround Formal?" Kat asked as they cut across the front lawn and headed over to the stadium. The Turnaround Formal was the annual girl-ask-boy dance. It was as popular as the senior prom.

"I didn't have to ask. We're just going," Miranda admitted, nudging Kat as the fields came into view, two ovals the color of polished emeralds. Eric was the new development in Miranda's life. Now that she and Eric were a couple, Kat was left out of a lot of things.

Kat kicked the grass. "Gee, if I didn't have to ask a guy, or do anything but just show up, maybe I'd go to the Turnaround Formal, too."

Miranda reminded herself of her next thing-to-do, then smiled. "I knew you wanted to go to that dance. I knew you were finally going to get sick of just cracking jokes and being buddy buddy with Gabe."

"Yeah. So what?" Kat laughed. "So maybe I *would* like to have a normal social life again — whatever normal is. What am I going to do about it? Have a personality transplant?"

"You'll see." As they walked past the practice field and the score board, Miranda heard the Junior Varsity coach's whistle, the low voices, and the smacks of the shoulder pads. She picked up her pace, energized by the sense of purpose on the field. The varsity field was quiet, however.

Since they had such an important game the next night, their practice must have ended early.

Miranda walked Kat down along the front of the bleachers. There were a lot of students still hanging around, plus parents, teachers, and a few middle-school kids. Everybody was making predictions for the upcoming game while Sarah Donovan, the photographer for *Bay News*, the school paper, was shooting pictures of the coach.

Miranda waved to Sarah and waited at the edge of the field. Close up, the grass wasn't such a perfect shade of green. Muddy patches had shown up near the goalposts, and the chalk sideline marks were faded and smeared. But when Miranda looked toward the gym, she saw someone who never seemed anything less than perfectly polished and bright.

"JAMISON!"

It was Eric Geraci, jogging across the field, lugging a pile of books that didn't seem to slow him down. Both powerful and graceful, Eric was a senior with dark hair cut short, framing his handsome, clean-cut face. Like the rest of his team who'd won by guts and discipline, he wasn't bulky or even all that big. He wore a red-and-white letterman's jacket, white shirt, crisp Levi's, and cowboy boots.

As soon as he reached the bleachers, Eric dropped his books and Miranda put down her briefcase. Then he scooped her off the ground, spinning and cradling her while she pressed her face against his warm, bare neck. She took in the scent of spicy after-shave, the pressure of his arms, and the feel of his cool, wet hair against the side of her face.

When Eric finally put her down, his brown eyes crinkled and his easy smile appeared.

"You two are embarrassing!" Kat covered her face and stomped her feet. "I think Gabe and I are going to have to make up characters like you for one of our radio routines." She put on a funny voice. "I'm Have-It-All Hannah and this is my sweetie, Hunky Hal."

Eric nudged her. "Kat, you'd better hold the jokes until you see what we have in store for you."

"What?"

Miranda held her breath. "Eric, did you arrange it?"

Eric nodded.

"Arrange what?" Kat asked.

"You'll see."

"You'll find out."

They both started pushing Kat back to the bleachers.

"Is this so bad that I have to be sitting down?"

"Don't worry, Kat."

"Just remember, we are your loving friends," Miranda reminded.

"So why do I feel like I'm about to be executed?"

They all plopped down on the bottom bleacher, a few rows below Sarah Donovan, who was changing the film in her camera. Miranda and Eric pressed in against Kat like bookends.

Eric nodded. "Here's the deal, Kat. You have a blind date this Saturday night with Michael Wexler. He'll pick you up at seven. You two can go out and then meet us later over at the Wave Cafe."

"Who's Michael Wexler?" Kat panicked.

"Michael Wexler?" Miranda echoed. When she'd asked Eric to fix Kat up, she'd assumed that he'd find someone wacky, like Gabe. She barely knew Michael, but he didn't seem like Kat's type.

"He's great," Eric insisted.

Miranda saw the sureness on Eric's face and

told herself that he was right. Michael was driven and good-looking, on the tennis team, and planning to study business in college. "You can't say no, Kat. You're going."

Kat fretted. She played with her necklace. She kicked her desert boots and bit her lip. "Oh, all right," she finally grumbled. "I know I should tell you both to go swim with the sharks, but I guess I'll give it a try. Just don't expect anything."

"Yayyyyyy!"

"Go for it, Kat!"

Miranda and Eric jumped up and shook each other's hands while Kat hunched over and moaned. Finally Eric threw his arms around Miranda again and pulled her close. "Enough of this handshaking, Miranda." He grinned, closing his eyes and leaning in to kiss her.

Miranda leaned her head back and felt his soft mouth against hers. But just as she was starting to get woozy with the feel of Eric's hand in her hair and his lips touching hers, Sarah Donovan jumped up behind them with her newspaper camera raised.

"Hold that!" Sarah yelled.

"What?" said Miranda, pulling away from Eric and blinking in confusion.

"I think she wants you to smooch again so she can take your picture," Kat teased.

"It's for the next issue of the newspaper," Sarah informed them. "I'll call it, 'Couple of the Year.'"

"Great!" Eric cheered, pulling Miranda in for another kiss. She resisted. "'Couple of the Year.' What a great name! Don't you think so, Miranda?"

Miranda stared at Eric's bright, handsome face, then looked down to take in Kat's worried smile. She didn't answer. For some weird reason, she was starting to get that unsteady feeling again.

TWO

"'Bye, Michael. Thanks for the . . ."

On Saturday night Kat jumped down from the front seat of Michael Wexler's brand-new pickup. The minute her desert boots hit the wooden planks of the Crescent Bay pier — before she'd even had a chance to say *Thanks for nothing, you bozo* — Michael pulled the door closed and drove away.

"Same to you, bud!" Kat called out after him.

She backed into a shadow and hugged her arms. She was standing on the pier under the squiggly neon light that marked the entrance to the Wave Cafe. The ocean lapped beneath her, and a few old men were still dangling their fishing poles. It was only eight-twenty. Her blind date had been awfully short.

"AHHHHHH!" Kat groaned, bending over and then stifling her voice by clapping her hands over her mouth. What was she going to tell Miranda? Her date had been a total flop. A disaster. Things couldn't have gone worse.

Just then the door to the Wave Cafe flew open, and hot, Saturday night music tumbled out. There was laughter, too. Boy-and-girl laughter that mingled together and was a perfect fit. Kat moved away quickly until she was standing at the edge of the pier, looking down into the dark, rolling water. The wind ruffled her short hair. The smell of salt comforted her. The sound of the waves made her think.

Even if the date hadn't worked out, maybe Miranda and Eric had been right to make Kat go. So she'd been hurt last summer. Kat knew she couldn't live through two more years of high school as if she'd declared war on the opposite sex. There was too much that she would miss: formals and parties, grad night and walking hand in hand on the beach.

Still, that didn't change her big problem. It was only eight-twenty. What was she going to tell Miranda? Where was she going to go to avoid showing up so early at the Wave? If she came in this early her friends would *know* her date had been a disaster.

Kat decided that the only answer was to take

a nice long walk down the pier. As she passed the old men with their fishing poles, she looked out at the dark, frothy water and sang softly to herself.

"Itsy-bitsy tiny ones. Think I'll eat some worms."

Inside the Wave Cafe, the Saturday night party partied on. Laughter echoed. Music hopped. Fishing nets hung from the timbered ceilings, dotted with sand dollars, pennants, and prom tickets. Noisy pinball machines blinked, while the statue of King Neptune overlooked it all in his red-and-white Crescent High letter sweater.

"Listen to me, Gabe," Jojo Hernandez was saying as she twisted her cheerleading charm around a painted fingernail. Her hair ended at her shoulders in tight curls, and her dark eyes sparkled. "Everyone's been talking about it. Junior year is getting really out of control."

"Life is out of control," Gabe joked. "Just ask Chip."

"Cosmic, Jojo," Chip Kohler agreed. "Cosmic and totally out of control."

"I'm serious, you two!" Jojo giggled. She pointed at Miranda. "Miranda, didn't you tell me, that Kat told you, that Turnaround Formal or no Turnaround Formal, no girl likes having to ask a guy out?"

Before Miranda could answer, Gabe had begun to tease. "Girls love asking *me* out." He tossed an ice cube at Miranda. "Besides, Miranda and Eric are the one couple on the planet who don't have to worry about getting asked out," Gabe used his glass as a microphone. "Miranda Jamison and Eric Geraci. Too good to be true. Are they real, or are they Memorex?" Then he tapped the glass with a spoon while they all sat forward and listened.

Brriiiiinnnng.

Gabe grinned at Miranda, but Miranda glanced back at Eric. She couldn't get into the jokey spirit of things. Thinking about the Turnaround Formal didn't seem as important as worrying about Kat. Nevertheless, she made an effort to take her mind off Kat's date and really be there with her friends.

"Don't look so smug, Miranda," Jojo teased, tapping Miranda's foot under the table. "Just because you and Eric are going to be together forever. And just because the football team is still undefeated!" She gave Eric a fervent thumbs up.

Eric flicked soda at her, which escalated into a lettuce-throwing contest and a cheese war, only ending when Eric defeated Gabe in a toothpick swordfight.

Miranda had to smile now. With her friends it was impossible not to. *The Voice, the Mouth, and the Hair* — as she and Kat referred to Gabe, Jojo, and Chip. Gabe was the Voice, because his witty deejay persona was imitated all over school, as were his flirty come-on lines and his radio characters. Muscular and curly haired, he wore a tight T-shirt, black jeans, and white high-tops every single day, turning his lack of money into a personal fashion statement. Jojo was the Mouth because, besides being an enthusiastic cheerleader, she had a stunning five-hundred-watt smile and an impressive lust for gossip. And they'd nicknamed Chip the Hair, because everything about him was soft and sixties, and his shoulder-length blond locks were the envy of every girl in the junior class.

"Go ahead and laugh now," Miranda teased back, touching one of her tiny diamond earrings. "But just wait until Monday when I whip you all into shape during our class assembly when we have to work on the quad project."

Gabe pretended to cower. "No. Please, no. I

almost forgot about the assembly on Monday. Not the quad project. Go easy on us, Miranda."

Chip held his napkin in front of his sensitive face. "I'll give up my Beatles albums and my tie-dyed T-shirts. Only please, don't whip me into shape!"

"I won't tell anyone our long-lost secrets from when we took sixth-grade gymnastics together," Jojo promised. "I promise, we'll be good!"

Miranda snuggled against Eric, while on the other side Jojo, Gabe, and Chip dove to grab the plastic containers shaped like tomatoes and glop ketchup over each other's curly Wave fries. There was finally a lull in the conversation, while they attacked their food.

Eric took a sip of his soda and leaned into Miranda. "Hey, I bet Michael and Kat are engaged by now."

The smile dropped off Miranda's face. Maybe she was superstitious, but she didn't want to hear anything that might jinx Kat's date. "Don't even say that," she told Eric in a low, serious voice.

"Miranda, stop worrying," Eric whispered, while keeping up his public smile.

"I'm not worrying," Miranda whispered back.

"You are, too. Kat's fine." Eric put his chin on Miranda's shoulder. "I still can't believe we won that game last night. I can't believe nobody had been able to beat us."

Miranda nodded. "I just keep wondering about Michael Wexler."

"He's fine," Eric stressed. "Forget about Kat, Miranda. We're here to have fun. Just relax."

Miranda's father said the same thing. She worried too much. She didn't know how to relax. "Okay. You're right."

Trying to ease up, she kissed Eric's cheek, then sat forward and took in the banter that was flying between her three friends again. But Miranda didn't join in. She didn't touch her food. That lost, unsteady feeling was tugging at her again, and this time she knew it wasn't going away. She sat up even taller and scanned the Wave crowd. She took in the sophomore surfer crowd, and red-haired Lisa Avery's notorious gang of senior girls, all of whom were trying to act as sexy and outrageously flirty as Lisa herself. Miranda saw Crescent Bay High couples and loners and some obvious weekend tourists. But the one person she was looking for was still nowhere in sight.

Eric suddenly got up. He had spotted his

teammate Alex Corley and wanted to go over and talk football. "I'll be right back," he said.

Miranda nodded.

Eric squeezed her shoulder, then left. Miranda was glad that they wouldn't talk about Kat's date for a while, even if she knew she couldn't stop thinking about it. That's when she heard Gabe's voice.

"Kat's not here yet, Miranda," Gabe whispered pointedly. He'd scooted to the end of the table, separating himself from Jojo and Chip, who were still bantering about the Turnaround dance. His usual joking tone was gone. "And that Michael Wexler guy is wrong for her."

Miranda showed her surprise. "Gabe, how did you know that Eric and I fixed Kat up on a blind date with Michael?"

"Kat called me this morning. You know, Kat talks to me almost as much as she talks to you," Gabe answered.

Something about Gabe's matter-of-factness made Miranda bristle. "How would you know who's right for anybody, anyway?" she told him as she stole the pickle off his plate. "You only flirt with every girl in school."

"I can't help it. They flirt with me." Gabe grinned. "Not everyone can be destined for greatness and only liking each other, like you and Eric." He craned his neck to see the Wave front door. "Besides, I know Kat. I don't flirt with Kat. But I know Michael is too intense for her."

Miranda pitched forward, taking a deep breath, until Gabe held his hand up and interrupted her, "Don't say it, Miranda. I know. There's no such thing as too intense."

Miranda managed to smile, even though every muscle in her tall, slender body was getting taut, as if she were about to jump out of her perfect, pale skin.

Just at that moment Gabe shot to his feet. He'd jumped up so quickly and so energetically that Miranda thought he'd sat on something, until she looked up, too, and saw Kat stepping through the Wave's front door. Kat looked sheepish, with her head down, and her hands stuffed into the pockets of her shorts.

"YO! KAT! DUDETTE!!" Gabe shouted, his face breaking into a huge grin. Chip and Jojo looked up, too. From the other end of the room Eric whistled, but he stayed talking with Alex. Meanwhile Jojo waved, while Chip held up two fingers in a peace symbol.

"Over here!" Jojo called.

Miranda bobbed from side to side to get a better view. "Where's Michael?"

"I don't see him," Gabe said. "It looks to me like good old Kat is flying solo."

Miranda's heart sank. She saw Kat pass the flirty Lisa Avery gang, then stall by talking to two girls from the swim team. Miranda went over all the reasons why Kat's blind date should have been a spectacular success. She couldn't deny it — she wanted Kat's date to be a success almost as much as she'd wanted to be president of the junior class. It would make last summer go away and put everything in order again.

Kat finally tore herself away from her fellow swimmers and slowly approached the gang's table. Without looking at Miranda, she plopped down on Gabe's lap and started wolfing down his fries.

Jojo leaned over the table. "Kat. Tell all. I want every single detail."

Miranda sighed. "Oh, Kat. What happened?"

"You okay, partner?" Gabe asked Kat in a soft voice.

Kat nodded and leaned into him. Finally she stopped eating and looked around the table. "Do you all really want to know the gory details of my date with Michael?"

Jojo nodded eagerly.

Chip shrugged.

Miranda knew what was coming. All her goals and plans were going to be turned into another of Kat's comedy routines.

Sure enough, Kat sat up on Gabe's lap and held out her hands, as if she were launching into a stand-up act. She avoided Miranda's gaze. "Okay. Since all of us together have known each other a total of almost twenty years, I guess I can tell you all the truth."

Gabe nibbled her shoulder and made a funny face.

Jojo grinned.

"Tell us," Chip said. "Whatever happened, we're on your side."

Miranda folded her arms and sat back, as Kat began in a once-upon-a-time voice.

"My date with Michael Wexler, by Kathleen McDonough," Kat pronounced. "Part one. Michael goes on and on about tennis." She mimed an exaggerated yawn. "Part two. We play miniature golf. I beat him on every tee and bore him by going on about swimming and the radio station." Kat yawned again.

Miranda wanted to *scream*.

Kat still wouldn't meet Miranda's eye. "Part three. We're back in the dark parking lot after we leave the miniature golf course, the minutes tick by, and Michael doesn't start the car."

"Tick, tick, tick, tick," Gabe began to whisper.

Kat leaned against him. "Michael pretends to stretch, and puts his arm around my shoulder."

"The old pretend-to-stretch-and-put-your-arm-around-her-shoulder move." Gabe nodded.

"So I turn away and then turn back really fast, just as he leans toward me, and we get our signals totally crossed. . . ."

Gabe began to snicker.

Jojo was hanging on every word.

"And for the grand finale, I ram into him with my head and give him a bloody nose!"

"NO!" Jojo cried.

Chip put his hand to his nose.

Kat forced a laugh and threw up her hands. "Anyone who wants to hear anything more about my thrilling love life, just buy a ticket and get in line."

Gabe broke into applause, and pretty soon Jojo was laughing her head off. Even mild-mannered Chip cut loose, and his long hair swept in someone's ketchup. Kat tossed lettuce in the air and started laughing and laughing, as if she would never stop.

Miranda wanted to join in the crazy fun. She wanted to know what Eric thought about Kat's date, but he was still with Alex, going over last night's game. Everyone else kept on laughing and joking.

But Miranda couldn't joke. She couldn't laugh. Her insides felt like a storm, and the Wave wasn't where she was. The wave was what was going on inside her.

THREE

Miranda was in top form again on Monday, pulled together and taking her place in front of the Crescent Bay High junior class. Her hair was fastened back and French-braided with silver ribbon. Her notes had been neatly printed out on her father's word processor. She stood confidently on the auditorium stage while Gabe adjusted her microphone stand and the other two hundred plus members of the class acted like they'd just been let out of a cage.

"TESTING, ONE, A TWO, A ONE TWO THREE FOUR," Gabe crooned into the mike. Notebooks were being slung around. Seats were being swapped. Potato-chip bags were being popped, making quick, hollow *phooomps*.

Miranda leaned into the mike, too. "HI, EVERYBODY. IT'S GOOD TO SEE YOU ALL. WE HAVE SOMETHING VERY IM-

PORTANT TO DISCUSS TODAY!"

"You tell us, Miranda," someone yelled.

Someone else *shhhhed* the crowd.

Miranda glanced down at Kat, Jojo, and Chip, who were sitting on the floor in front of the first row. At least she and Kat had talked the day before and gone over the whole blind date again . . . and again and again and again. Miranda had finally agreed — she'd made a mistake. No more dates. Even though Eric hadn't admitted that Michael might have been a bad idea, the case was pretty much closed.

"LET'S GET SETTLED AS QUICKLY AS WE CAN," Miranda commanded.

Gradually the auditorium quieted.

"Mr. Shorestein," Miranda introduced. She gestured down to where their adviser still stood in the side doorway. When Mr. Shorestein was convinced that there were no more stragglers in the hall, he pulled the side door closed and marched up. Gabe handed the mike over with a salute, then jumped down and squeezed in between Kat and Jojo.

"Greetings all," Mr. Shorestein droned. "I'll get right to the point here. As most of you know, the student population of Crescent Bay High is on the rise, as is the population of Crescent Bay as a whole. I'm sure you've all noticed that expensive new monster called the Tucker Resort down on Overlook Point."

Chip called out, "How could you miss it?"

A gum bubble exploded, followed by laughter.

Mr. Shorestein frowned. "The Tucker Resort is just one example of how our quaint, little town is no longer quite so quaint or so little. Crescent Bay has been discovered, and we need to adjust to our growing population." Mr. Shorestein took a step away from the mike. "Here's your hardworking president. She'll tell you what you can do to help."

Miranda stepped up. Gabe wolf-whistled. Jojo applauded as if it were a first down. Chip smiled sweetly, and Kat raised her fist in support.

"Thank you, Mr. Shorestein," Miranda stated, bolstered by her friends. She looked straight at her class without a blink or a smile. "We all know that funding has been voted to remodel our cafeteria."

Gabe called out something about remodeling the food. Kat elbowed him while Jojo laughed.

"Since they're going to be working on our caf," Miranda went on, "we've decided that it would be a good time to fix up our quad as well.

Unfortunately we don't have enough funding
for a new quad. The Crescent Bay Bank guar-
anteed to match the money we raise ourselves."

Whispers trickled across the auditorium.

"Each class needs to come up with four
hundred dollars," Miranda clarified, her voice
bouncing off the back wall. "Any ideas on how
to raise the money?"

Feeling sure and in control, Miranda waited
for the first suggestion. At the same time, she
took in her class. Even though Crescent Bay
High wasn't a big school, all the classic types
were represented. There were some really rich
kids and some poor ones, too, plus brains and
jocks, soshes and nerds, and a few out-and-out
weirdos. Miranda and her friends didn't fall into
any crowd category. Her house had been fea-
tured in *Design Magazine*, while Gabe lived in a
trailer park. Jojo was wildly popular, but Kat
was sort of an oddball. Eric was an all-American
jock, while Chip baked his own bread.

Miranda was still marveling at the uniqueness
of her friends when she realized that several
hands were waving. But before she could call on
anyone, a boy in the second row shot to his feet.
Every muscle in Miranda's body clenched.

"I think we might be ahead of ourselves, here," the boy mentioned, gesturing to the kids around him. "Can we find out if we're all for this quad fix-up before we plan to raise money for it?"

Miranda tried to keep a smile on her face as she stared at Jackson Magruder, editor of *Bay News*, the school paper. This wasn't an unsteady feeling, but a preparation for getting tossed by a huge wave. "Excuse me?"

Jackson locked onto her with big, green eyes. He was lanky and long-legged with short, almost punk brown hair and a slightly crooked smile that everyone else took for pure charm. Miranda wasn't impressed. Not by his relaxed air, his quirky grin, or his leather bomber jacket. Besides being head of the newspaper, Jackson was a Friends in Need peer counselor. Everyone thought he was so hip and insightful. Everyone except Miranda.

"I said, who decided that we want to raise money to fix up the quad at all?" Jackson repeated.

Miranda stood tall. "We had a meeting, and that's what we came up with."

"A meeting? Who had this meeting?" Jackson

asked easily. "How many people were at this meeting? Twelve? A hundred and twelve? Just you?"

Miranda wanted to say, *Look, Jackson. Just because you redid the newspaper and changed it from a boring throwaway to a radical rag that people stand in line for, that doesn't mean you can ruin my assembly. I put a lot of planning into this, a lot of worry and hard work!* "There were four of us, all the class presidents."

Jackson still hadn't taken his eyes off her. "Four of you. That sounds like a real majority."

People laughed.

Miranda glanced down. Jojo seemed annoyed. Chip looked thoughtful. Gabe got up on his knees, and Kat stared.

"Jackson, is there something wrong with fixing up our quad?" Miranda demanded.

"Nothing's wrong with a better quad, Miranda," Jackson challenged. "But if we work to raise money, maybe that's not what we want to spend it on. We shouldn't have to do something just because you want it."

Miranda felt something come loose inside her. That was another thing that had been happening to her lately. Besides the lost feeling, it didn't take much to make her lose her cool. "People like to eat outside. We have great weather here. A nicer quad would get a lot of use."

A burst of applause backed her up.

Jackson clapped, too, then added. "So would a pinball machine in the attendance office."

Equal applause.

"What?"

"A telescope in the parking lot," Jackson suggested.

Hoots of approval.

"Come on, Jackson."

"A swimming hole on the front lawn with a tire swing and a waterfall."

Whistles and more applause.

"Thank you, Jackson. It's always great to get new ideas. Anything else?"

Jackson thought for a moment. If her crowd was hard to put into a category, Jackson was impossible. Sometimes he rode a skateboard like a surf punk, but he got A's. Girls were wild for him, but he rarely dated. And he wrote the most bizarre feature stories for the paper. Things like what had ever happened to Mr. Potato Head, or what the world would look like if the sky weren't blue. Despite his popularity, he was the kind of person her father would say was "on the fringe."

"I have nothing else to say," Jackson finally decided. "Thanks for letting me talk. I think I've made my point."

After that, Miranda took a careful vote, making sure that the quad plan was indeed backed by a majority. It was. Almost everyone voted for it, including Jackson. And yet, Jackson's objection had completely changed the mood. After the vote, everyone giggled and talked to each other, but no one ventured a single fund-raising idea.

"Let's just throw some fund-raising suggestions out there," Miranda urged. "This is for a very important cause."

Finally Jojo saved the day by turning her sparkly smile on the crowd. She jumped up and waved the notebook in which she kept track of new cheerleading routines. "How about a candy-bar drive?"

Thank you, Jojo, Miranda thought. "That's good!"

There were a few encouraging murmurs.

Kat popped up, too. "How about a swim-athon?"

Other juniors began to join in.

"How about a bake sale?"

"A carnival?"

"Those are terrific ideas," Miranda encouraged, silently thanking her friends for never letting her down.

Jojo waved her list again. "Okay, okay, here's another idea!" She had that excited look she got at the end of Eric's winning football games. "How about a car wash?!"

When there was no immediate response, Jojo's smile faded, and Miranda decided to make the decision for them. "Let's vote on this," Miranda commanded. "The sooner we make a plan, the earlier we all get to go eat lunch. All opposed to a car wash?"

A few groans and hand claps.

"All in favor of a car wash?"

"YAAAAAAAAAAAAAAYYYYY!!!!!!!!!"

"Okay, Jojo," Miranda finished, forgoing any of the other suggestions. "That's it. A car wash it is!"

As soon as Miranda said it, people started to stand up. Mr. Shorestein yelled for them to form a line at the door, and they began to file out.

Miranda spoke slowly into the microphone. "We're going to need lots of help, so everyone please check the activity bulletin board."

Half her class was already gone, but the other half was looking up, nodding in approval.

Kat had stopped at the edge of the stage and leaned over to tap Miranda's toe. "Miranda."

Miranda looked down.

"See you at Jojo's locker," Kat said, referring to the lunch spot where their group had met for the last three semesters.

"I'll be there soon." Miranda waved to Gabe, Chip, and Jojo, who were almost out the door. "I just have to turn out the stage lights."

"Okay. Meet you at Jojo's locker." Kat joined the rest of the juniors filing out in record time.

Soon Miranda was left alone with the smell of dust and old wood, the faded wall murals of waves and fishing boats, and the new scenery for the upcoming musical.

Already making mental lists about assigning people to locate car wash equipment and print fliers, Miranda walked to the side of the stage. There she found the large metal box with red levers that looked like a toy robot. Miranda was reading the small labels, trying to remember which switch would turn off which bank of lights, when she heard footsteps. Looking back over her shoulder, she froze. Even though she saw little more than a shadow backed by a heavy velvet curtain and a few old wooden chairs, every ounce of her being was ready for a fight.

"Jackson," she cursed in a low voice.

"Excuse me," he whispered.

You are not excused! Miranda thought, grabbing another red plastic handle on the light machine and flinging it to OFF. Don't give me yet another stupid suggestion and any more of your I'm-the-only-one-with-any-originality charm. Don't blame me for railroading the class into accepting Jojo's idea. If you don't like it, come up with something better!

But then Miranda glanced back again, catching the boy this time and not the shadow. Her heart slowed down again, and she had a flash that it was Eric, since the boy was tall and his shoulders were wide. She wondered if Eric finally wanted to apologize for Michael Wexler. But then she looked harder and realized this boy was even leaner than Eric and more refined — the difference between a football end and a boy who sailed boats or raced thoroughbred steeds.

He stepped forward into the light and stuck out his hand in an almost courtly gesture. Two deep dimples appeared when he smiled a reserved, paper-white smile. His hair was blond with a few goldish streaks, short on the sides, long and straight on top so that it flopped over one eye. He wore a striped shirt, navy suspenders, and crisp khaki trousers, as if he'd just stepped off the cover of a preppy clothes catalog.

Miranda didn't mean to stare, but she was off balance again. He didn't look like any other boy at Crescent Bay High. And he didn't throw his individuality in her face, like Jackson Magruder. He just stood there with the indefinable air of someone who had to be extraordinary.

"Hello. I'm Miranda Jami — " she began.

He interrupted, shaking his head as if she were so famous that everyone already knew who she was. "I know who you are. I'm a junior, too. I just sat through this assembly." He took her hand and held it in a respectful, serious way. "Nice to meet you. I just transferred here, and I want to introduce myself. I'm Brent Tucker."

Brent Tucker! *He* was the famous one. "As in the new Tucker Resort?" Miranda made sure. Jojo had heard rumors that the fabulously wealthy Tucker family included a teenaged son and that he might transfer to Crescent Bay High.

Brent seemed embarrassed by the connection. He looked down at his deck shoes, worn with argyle socks. "I guess. I mean, yes, of course, my parents built the Tucker Resort. But I hope I can be known for something besides the huge building my parents stuck on what must have been a pretty spectacular ocean cliff." He shook his head. "What did Mr. Shorestein call my parents' resort? A monster?"

"I think that was the word he used." Miranda didn't add that lots of Crescent Bay old-timers had been complaining about the new, glitzy complex. Although, as her dad had pointed out, the Tucker Resort was sure to bring in more tourism, which meant better business and bigger bucks. "I wouldn't worry about it. I'm sure he didn't mean anything by it."

"I'm sure he did."

Neither of them said anything for a moment. They just stood staring at each other as muffled lunch noises rose and the wooden floor creaked.

"Anyway," Brent said, "I just wanted to tell you that I'd like to help the class in some way. What can I do?"

Not only was Brent charming, great-looking, and polite, he wanted to help! "Just check the activity board, the one I mentioned outside the guidance office," Miranda gushed. "Everything that's happening is posted on that board."

"Okay. I'll do that." He clapped his hands together and checked his watch. "Well, I'd better go. I'm supposed to meet with my counselor and make sure my classes are okay."

"Of course. Welcome to Crescent Bay."

"Thanks."

"Nice to meet you."

"You, too."

He walked down the steps, while Miranda watched him go. Brent was the type of guy even her dad would approve of. No boy had made such an overwhelming impression on her since Eric. Actually, if it weren't for Eric, she might have been interested in him. But she prided herself in being loyal, and she really wasn't tempted. Besides, she wasn't thinking about herself. She was thinking about Kat again.

FOUR

"Hi, Jojo!"

"Great idea for the car wash, Jojo!"

"I saw you at the game last Friday night, Jojo. The squad is looking good!"

"Jojo, I have to talk to you during sixth period. I have some really good dirt about the Turnaround dance."

"OKAY!" Jojo Hernandez smiled and waved to the people passing by, then turned back to her locker. It was no wonder that her friends met there for lunch almost every day. Her locker was in a great location — in the outdoor hallway just beyond the library, right next to the overcrowded quad. A metal picnic table was only a few feet away, along with a retaining wall that was the perfect height to sit on, watch the action, and easily join in.

"Car wash!" Jojo grinned, congratulating her-

self on the assembly as she proudly posted yet
another note inside her locker door. While waiting for her friends, she scribbled a few more
phrases.

> *Tell everyone about it.*
> *Find out what they all really think!*

Other people had pictures of rock stars taped
to the insides of their lockers. Jojo had notes.
Times for cheerleading practice. Invitations to
parties and fliers about social activities. As her
dad said — *people* were what it was all about.

Jojo sorted through her locker until she found
her lunch, which she packed to ensure good skin
and zero weight gain. Pulling out the decorated
pink sack, Jojo rearranged the rest of her locker
belongings — mirror, dictionary, nail polish,
and computer manual — to find a place for her
French book. That was when she felt Chip creep
up behind her.

Chip gave her curly hair a tug.

"Hi!" She grinned up at him.

"Very cool assembly." Chip smiled as he un-
packed his lunch on top of the table. He'd
brought sesame crackers, cookies, juice, and an
avocado sandwich. "A car wash is a good idea.

A waste of water, but a good idea."

"Thanks." Jojo blushed. She was sailing on the knowledge that her suggestion had been the final choice. "Miranda's the one who made it happen. I would never have the nerve to stand up there and stare the class down the way she does."

Chip nodded and peered across the quad. Lunch was in full swing. The air was warm, and the sun poked through a few slow-moving clouds. "Where is everybody?"

Jojo kept rearranging the contents of her locker as she waved to a trio of seniors. "Miranda must still be closing up the auditorium, and Eric just isn't here yet. Kat went to get something in the caf. Gabe is probably borrowing quarters so he can buy lunch, too. They'll all be here soon."

"Okay."

Jojo had finally managed to stow her French text when her computer class manual started to tumble out. She gasped and leaned back against the locker next to hers, which belonged to a spooky loner type named Leanne Heard, who sat next to Jojo in English. Leanne was the type that made Jojo want to get down on her knees in thanks for her popularity and her friends.

Flattening herself against Leanne's locker, Jojo

caught her computer manual by its cover, but the book flopped open and a piece of folded notebook paper floated to the ground.

Chip scooped it up before Jojo could get it.

"I'll take that," Jojo blurted out, her smile becoming a little forced.

"What is it?"

"Nothing!" Jojo didn't want to admit that she had other notes, besides the ones publicly plastered on her locker door. Private notes. Notes about who had crushes on whom, about who was asking whom to the Turnaround Formal, and who she might consider asking out herself.

"What is it, Jojo?"

Jojo tried to laugh.

"Come on. You tell Miranda and Kat everything. From what I've seen, you tell all the other girls everything, too."

"I do not!" Jojo did have a hard time keeping her mouth shut, but she considered that a virtue. Who else would tell girls when their boyfriends were cheating or their best friends had been untrue? Jojo snatched the paper out of Chip's hand. "It's just this silly list we made on the computer, the names of guys that the girls in my class are thinking of asking to the dance." She stuck the paper back into her locker.

"Sorry." Chip went back to his sandwich until his soft features suddenly lit up. "Wait a minute. Like, is my name on there?"

"Sure, Chip," Jojo blabbed without thinking. "Six of us listed our top three choices, and you were on the top of every list. Lisa Avery is going to ask you to the dance."

Chip brushed the long hair away from his face and leaned forward. "Lisa mentioned me?"

Jojo saw the seriousness in his eyes and felt like banging her head against Leanne's locker door. "Chip, that list is private."

"Come on, Jojo."

Why couldn't she ever keep her mouth shut! Girls weren't romantically interested in Chip, especially a notorious senior flirt like redheaded Lisa. Maybe it was because he was *too* nice, too sixties mellow.

Jojo took a deep breath. "Oh, um, Lisa *is* in my class, but I don't know what she thinks about you." She closed her locker and patted him. "But from what I've heard about Lisa, you're probably better off without her." She gave him a quick hug.

Chip turned away from her, then thoughtfully picked at his lunch. Jojo opened her cottage cheese and tried to eat, too, but the confusion

with Chip had taken some of the spark out of
her car wash high.

Luckily just at that moment Miranda and Eric
appeared to brighten things up again. They were
strolling arm in arm, slightly out of step, but
looking like two fresh-faced models in a health
class film about high self-esteem.

"It's Iron Man," said Chip. "And the Million-
Dollar Miranda."

"Hi, you guys!" Jojo cheered.

As soon as Eric arrived, he did a ridiculous
handshake with Chip, then picked up Jojo
around the waist, almost as if she were a football.
Meanwhile, Miranda sat down at their table with
a funny secret smile.

A moment later, Gabe appeared, too, cutting
through the quad with Kat. He took a detour,
dancing around a couple of awestruck freshmen while Kat trotted over and plopped down
across from Miranda. Soon all six of them were
digging into their lunches and talking at the
same time.

"Sorry we took so long," said Kat. "The caf
is so — "

"OVERCROWDED," Jojo and Gabe sang.
"Really."

Gabe laughed. "Pretty soon we're going to

have to get in line by first period just to buy a carton of milk."

"Maybe we should do a routine about that on the radio," Kat suggested. "Three's a crowd in the overcrowded quad."

Gabe nodded. "Good idea, buddy."

Eric took big bites of his first hamburger and leaned in. "You know, we had our senior overcrowding assembly this morning, too."

"I heard you had an assembly," said Jojo. "I want to know everything that happened."

Eric smirked. "Lisa Avery suggested a kissing booth."

Jojo's mouth fell open. "No!"

Chip choked.

"What's the matter, guy?" Gabe asked, slapping Chip on the back.

"Why is everybody talking about Lisa all of a sudden?" Chip asked.

"Who said anything about Lisa?" Gabe nudged Kat and added in a Groucho voice, "Not that Lisa isn't worth talking about."

"I think a kissing booth is insulting," Kat objected.

"Why?" asked Gabe.

"Because it's always the girls who are selling the kisses," Kat pointed out.

"Maybe I should have volunteered to sell kisses at our assembly," Gabe joked. "I bet we'd make a fortune."

Kat rolled her eyes.

Eric gave Miranda's cheek a peck. "Don't worry, Kat. The seniors decided on decorating windows for downtown businesses instead."

Miranda smiled.

"Good." Kat thought for a minute, then switched sandwich halves with Gabe and began to eat. They all munched while the clouds shifted and the sun shined through.

After they had all finished at least a third of their food, Miranda opened her notebook, as if it were a meeting of the board. Everyone leaned forward, the way they always did when Miranda took the lead. But for once, Miranda didn't quite look at them.

"Okay, everybody," Miranda began in a slightly evasive voice. "Now that we've decided on this car wash, we have to plan everything out." She jotted something down and pointed at Jojo. "Jojo, can you make a flier for me in Melman's computer class?"

Jojo nodded, taking her task with utmost seriousness.

"I'll need it by this Friday's game," Miranda

ordered. "We have less than two weeks to get this together."

"I'll do it," Jojo promised, already trying to think of catchy phrases and a good layout design.

"I'll find out about equipment." Miranda turned her attention to Gabe and Kat. But once again, she didn't quite meet their eyes. "So, do you think we can promote the car wash on the radio?"

"Sure. We still have some free airtime this Friday," Kat offered.

Gabe nodded. "Is this Friday okay?"

Miranda didn't respond. Instead she clicked the point in and out of her pen. Then she doodled aimlessly, something Jojo had never seen her do before. They all watched her.

"Actually I wanted to ask you to add something else to Friday's show, or rather someone else," Miranda finally said. "Do you have time to interview another person on Friday?"

"Who? Jackson Magruder?"

Miranda flinched. "No, Gabe. Definitely not Jackson."

"Who then?" asked Kat. "We have a student council interview set up with Roslyn Griff, but we can squeeze in a minute or two with someone else."

Miranda didn't answer. Instead, she stared down at her notebook and seemed to be hiding a smile. Jojo knew that something was up. She had no idea what it was, and she was dying to find out.

"Thanks," Miranda finally decided, leaning back against Eric and giving him a quick kiss. Then she grinned at Kat. "I'll just bring the person over to the station on Friday."

Kat stared at Miranda, then shrugged. "Okay."

After that the talk started flying at supersonic speed again. Miranda was her old intense self, planning the car wash, while Eric made predictions of another win for Friday's football game, and Chip went on about biodegradable car soap. Gabe managed to make Kat laugh so hard she fell off the bench. And the whole time, Jojo thought about her car-wash flier and reminded herself how lucky she was to have five such fabulous friends.

Friend.
1. *A person bound to another person by strong feelings of affection.*
2. *A supporter.*
3. *One who is not hostile.*

At the other end of the corridor, past the open library door, Leanne Heard stood with her English class dictionary poised over an overflowing trash can.

"Hostile," Leanne scoffed. She wanted to laugh as she stared down at Jojo and her friends. "You bet I'm hostile! I am not a supporter of your stupid car wash. And I don't have strong feelings for any of you. Not when you won't even let me get to my own stupid locker!"

Leanne resisted the urge to throw her dictionary away. Maybe she was hostile, but she wasn't stupid — no matter what popular Jojo and her crowd thought. The dictionary had been issued in English class, and Leanne wasn't going to get hit up for a lost book fee.

"At least you could let me get to my locker so I could throw it in there," Leanne muttered. "But, no."

Finally she pitched the dictionary back in her sack, which she'd sewn out of remnants of velvet found at a local thrift store. She couldn't believe she'd been reduced to reading her stupid dictionary just so people wouldn't think she looked conspicuous while trying to plan a route to her own locker.

Like I really care what people think, Leanne

tried to tell herself. She was proud of being an outsider, as long as she could stay outside, and not be inside their catty gossip. Leanne was her own person. The last thing she wanted to become was the object of chitchat for those busy, big-mouthed, popular girls.

Leanne flattened against the library wall and looked back down the hall. Sure enough, the royal court was still holding their daily conference right in front of Leanne's private locker. Jojo Hernandez and her *friends*.

Leanne's rage started to bubble up as she strode past Jojo's lunch table. It was bad enough to sit through a whole assembly with those people, but now she didn't want to look any of them in the eye. Of course, they didn't look up at her, either, as she quickly passed. They just kept laughing and chattering and writing important lists in their important notebooks. Leanne left them behind, striding toward the main office and student parking lot. She wondered when she'd be able to sneak back to her locker and fetch her government book, which was required for fifth period.

Required. Designer aerobic shoes were probably required by Jojo and her popularity police, as were outfits that matched and makeup that looked "natural." Well, Leanne wasn't going for it. In worn leather moccasins, a secondhand forties dress and cowboy belt, she could be as proud of her sense of style as Jojo was of hers. Prouder. Leanne had bleached her hair platinum blonde knowing that it set off her creamy white skin. She wore the darkest red lipstick she could find, confident that she didn't look like any other girl at Crescent Bay High.

When Leanne got to the main school entrance, she stopped. The parking lot was full, and a few sea gulls were flapping their wings overhead. Some freshmen were playing Frisbee on the lawn. Leanne sat down beside the flagpole. She'd sit there until lunch was over, she decided. And she'd be late to fifth period.

Again.

"I have no choice," she said out loud. What could she do? Tell Ms. Dorris the dog ate her government book? Say she left her book at home?

The thought of home hit Leanne's stomach like a fast-pitched ball, and she leaned over, hugging her curvy body and letting out a tiny moan. It was a word that was almost as loaded for her as the word *friend*. She rested her cheek on her knee and stayed like that, even when the bell rang and everyone else started running to class.

Leanne didn't budge until after the tardy bell went off. She heard the door to the main office open behind her. Suspecting the hall patrol, she quickly grabbed her velvet bag and got up. Afraid of getting caught, she didn't take the most direct route back to her locker. Instead she scurried around the gym, past a janitor's shed, and over a bank of shrubs. She ended up just outside the guidance office, staring down a long empty hall.

For a moment Leanne was lost. She'd been at Crescent Bay High for two and a half years but for some reason she couldn't get her bearings. Then she looked again and saw the activity bulletin board. No wonder she hadn't recognized it. She'd probably wanted to block it out.

She stared at the glass-covered board with all its fliers and lists. The fact that the glass was locked always killed Leanne. It was as if people were going to sneak up and rearrange the names. Then the popular kids wouldn't know if they were in the Environmentalists or the Pep Club. Gee, maybe they'd have to go to Jojo and straighten everything out.

Leanne stared blankly at the board. Turnaround Formal. Fall musical. Quad project. Service Society. Decorating committee. Business Club. Friends in Need.

Leanne stepped closer.

Friends in Need? Maybe it was a group organized by Jojo for people who needed friends so badly they were actually skipping meetings and forgetting to say hi. Maybe it was just a cover to get more people to scrub cars and raise money for the quad.

Leanne felt something open up inside. Now that she thought about it, she remembered announcements about Friends in Need at the beginning of the term. Unlike the football games and dances, it wasn't one of those activities that people talked about every day. Almost no one mentioned the counseling program, where certain kids had been trained as peer helpers and were supposed to always be on call if any other students were falling apart.

Yeah, right, Leanne told herself, backing away from the board and looking out for hall patrol. The peer counselors were probably Popularity Princess Jojo, or Control Queen Miranda Jamison. The only one of the crowd that Leanne would ever want to talk to was Kat McDonough, and that was only because Kat sometimes said things over the radio that made Leanne smile. Actually, the more Leanne thought about it, the more she would never want to talk to a girl at all. Because girls made plans for you. They pretended to understand, and then one girl talked to another girl, who talked to another and . . .

And yet, Leanne couldn't quite leave the board. Her five-minute late warning was turning into a full-fledged tardy. The hall patrol was probably lurking around the corner. And yet she still stood and stared.

When Leanne still couldn't decide if Friends in Need was any more relevant than the car wash or the Pep Club, she pulled out her dictionary again and looked up the word *need*.

1. A strong desire.
2. Lack of something wanted, as in money.

It wasn't until Leanne read the third definition that she got that fast-pitch feeling in her stomach again.

Need:
3. A situation of extreme difficulty.

FIVE

"Kat, I need my headphones! Where are they?"

"Gabe, do you know that you always lose something just before our show goes on the air?"

"Kat, I do not always lose something. Where's my playlist? Look at the clock. We only have ninety-seven seconds before airtime."

"You do, too, always lose something, Gabe. Just before last week's show you lost the sound-effects box and before that you lost your sunglasses."

"I did?"

"I've never known why you wear your sunglasses on the air anyway."

"Kat, would you stop being so calm and help me find my stuff."

"Gabe, would you stop being so nervous and open your eyes."

"We're down to sixty-two seconds here."

"Gabe."

"Why is it that when I'm having a nervous breakdown is when you're suddenly all confident and chatty?"

"GABE."

"WHAT?"

"Here's your playlist."

"Where was it?"

"Right in front of you. And so were your headphones. Here."

During lunch on Friday, Kat swiveled in her chair and tossed Gabe's headphones across the tabletop, past the single microphone that sat between them in the closet-sized studio of the campus radio station, KHOT. Gabe held up his hands in a gesture of exaggerated thanks, slapped the earphones on, and began staring at the big wall clock.

"Thirty-two seconds." On went his shades. He slumped in his chair, undergoing his twice-weekly transformation from hyper, smart, funny Gabe Sachs in his tight T-shirt and black jeans, to cool, laid-back radio deejay in his shades.

Kat poised her hand over the ON THE AIR button. She was undergoing a transformation of her own. As the second hand on the station clock

ticked away, she sat up, crossing her legs underneath her, and leaning forward. She shook
her bangs away from her eyes. She tucked her
necklace inside her shirt — that day it held a
whistle, a pen, and a cartoon held on with a paper
clip. The closer they got to lift-off, the more
contained and grounded she felt.

Eighteen seconds.

"Gabe, are we going to split the mike first
thing, or should I make the announcements right
away?"

"What do you think?" Gabe whispered, his
hand over the mike as the clock counted down
the last twelve seconds. "You decide, partner."

"Let's start with a split mike," Kat decided.
"After that, I'll read the announcements, and
then you can do platter time."

"Sounds good to me."

"Let's run with it."

"Okay, buddy. Let's travel."

They both stared at the clock. "Split mike"
meant their routines, where their comic characters shared the air, carrying on about campus
events. Gabe had invented the term. Over the
last year as partners, Kat and Gabe had made up
lots of private jokes and weird names. "Platter
times" were Gabe's musical interludes, "genius

burger" was a good interview, and "dinosaur breath" was any routine or interview that turned out to be a dud.

Four seconds. Three . . .

They leaned toward the mike at the same time. Just before Kat pushed the ON THE AIR button she caught Gabe's eye. One curl had fallen over his forehead, and his handsome face had crinkled up in an excited smile. Kat felt something bubble up inside.

ON THE AIR.

"Hello, Sea Lions," Kat said in a voice that came out a little lower and more seductive than she'd intended.

Gabe made sea lion barks and nibbled her shoulder.

"It's totally hot at KHOT again today," Kat said, adding a husky Southern quality. She'd meant to start out as the uptight society lady, but her voice had come out as Patty Prom Queen instead, a Southern tease. She felt so free on the radio, that she could even sound sexy and not worry about it.

Gabe immediately picked up on her tone. He wheeled closer and put on his dorky lounge lizard character. "Hey, baby, haven't I seen you somewhere before?"

"I guess I do stand out in a crowd."

"Baby, you are a crowd. If you ask me, you qualify as an overcrowd. Hey, maybe that's where I met you. In the overcrowded Crescent Bay High cafeteria."

"Somewhere among the stuffed peppers."

"In the mashed potatoes."

"Around the freshly squeezed juice."

Kat worked to keep a straight face. She could feel the energy flipping between her and Gabe like a tennis ball.

"I'd never forget a mashed potato like you, baby," Gabe joked, his glasses slipping down his nose so she could see him wink. "I think I met you there with a friend. Didn't I?"

"I don't think so," Kat answered, preparing to get the last word. "You know what they say. Three's a crowd."

Gabe pushed a toggle switch on his homemade sound-effects box, sending the loud splat of an egg breaking on the floor. After that Kat pushed a switch that finished the segment with a triumphant female laugh.

They exchanged thumbs up. Then Kat launched into the first announcement about that night's football game while Gabe took off his sunglasses. He spun around and slipped that

show's CDs out of their cases. He was in charge
of the tunes, and he was great at it. He seemed
to know every jazz, rock, or pop song ever recorded. Kat was the one who'd introduced the
chitchat after she'd been assigned to write a radio
play for sophomore drama class. Gabe had
helped her with that broadcast, and the rest was
history.

Kat read off the rest of the announcements.
"Let's see. The Honor Society is meeting on
Monday in room 203. Friends in Need is going
to be training more counselors. Girls' B ball
starts next Thursday after school. . . ."

Meanwhile, Gabe swung back around, opening the CD cases and deciding which cuts he
wanted to play. He slapped a disc in each of the
two CD players in one graceful movement, then
scribbled a note and stuck it in front of Kat. *It's
almost platter time. P.S. Miranda's outside with her
mystery guest.*

Kat nodded. "And we don't want to forget
the junior car wash. That's all for now, Sea
Lions."

Gabe barked again.

"Here's Dr. Rock."

Gabe took over with his music while Kat patted him, then bounded out of her chair to greet

Miranda and the guest, who were waiting in the audiovisual room right next to the studio. Kat hadn't given much thought to Miranda's guest, because she'd been too busy thinking about her interview with Roslyn Griff, their student body president. But Roslyn had been sent home with the flu that morning. Still, Kat wasn't worried. Miranda never let anyone down. Her guest was probably head of the Honor Society or from the International Club.

"Miranda," Kat said, pushing the door open and letting it swing closed behind her. But as soon as she stepped into the audiovisual room she froze.

"Hi, Kat. I'd like you to meet Brent," Miranda said with icebox cool. "He's going to be your guest on the show today."

Everything inside Kat shut down, as if all her brain circuits had been disconnected. Brent was definitely not the self-important senior who ran the honor society. He might have been from the international club, except that Kat had never seen him before. He had goldish blond hair and a tan the color of freshly baked biscuits. He wore suspenders with a dark green turtleneck, jeans, and loafers. When he smiled at Kat, he didn't fidget. He didn't look away. His eyes took her in as if she were a jewel in a display case.

"Oh. Um. Yes." Kat stood there nodding like one of those dolls people put on their dash-boards.

"Brent, this is Kat McDonough," Miranda said in a purposeful voice. She smiled at Kat, and opened her eyes wide, sending some secret message.

Kat just stared.

"Kat," Brent repeated. He held out a hand to shake. "Nice to meet you. Is it really okay for me to be on your show? I'm new, and I sort of have an announcement. Miranda told me she thought this might be a good idea."

Kat transferred her stare to his palm when Miranda's smile set off an alarm inside her brain. Of course! Why hadn't she seen it coming when Miranda had arranged this mystery interview? This was another setup. No! She'd told Miranda that past Sunday, "I am what I am," as Popeye always said. I did what I did last summer, now I'll be an old maid, and there's nothing you can do about it. STOP MAKING PLANS!

When Kat still hadn't accepted his handshake, Brent laughed. He grabbed her hand and put it in his with mock seriousness.

Kat pumped his hand too hard.

"I don't know why I'm shaking hands," he said.

Kat laughed.

Brent laughed, too, and shook her hand even harder. "I'm acting like my father." He cringed. "I know I'm going to have to talk a little about my family on the show, but I don't want to dwell on it. Please. Will you promise me that?"

Kat was confused.

"Brent's family owns the new Tucker Resort," Miranda clarified.

"Brent *Tucker*?" Kat blurted out. The knowledge that he was a Tucker wiped out any speck of composure she might have had left. Only that morning Jojo had been gossiping about Brent's arrival! And Brent seemed to be everything Jojo's grapevine had said he was: gorgeous, together, polite, and charming.

Brent seemed embarrassed, too, but still didn't let go of Kat's hand.

Kat stared down, as aware of his touch as if he had just wrapped his arms around her. She might have stood there all lunch period, except that Gabe's voice suddenly pierced through her panic.

"Hello. Hello," Gabe was insisting. "Come in, Kat. Remember me? Remember KHOT? We're almost back on the air."

Kat flinched and pulled her hand away from Brent, locating Gabe who was standing in the studio doorway. He had one hand on the door frame and the other on his hip. A deep crease had formed over his eyebrows.

"So you're our guest for today," Gabe said to Brent in a cool voice. He looked back and forth from Miranda to Brent to Kat to Brent again. "Come on in."

Kat gave a quick look back to Miranda, then swallowed and followed Brent into the closet-sized studio.

SIX

"It was the right thing to do," Miranda said to herself as soon as she left the station and hurried to her next task. "I did it for Kat."

Although she kept her posture stiff as she passed the auditorium and the teachers' lounge, Miranda was mentally swinging back and forth. She'd been right to introduce Brent to Kat! No, she'd been devious. She'd promised Kat that she wouldn't set her up again. But Brent wasn't another Michael Wexler. Miranda thought of the advice her father always gave her before he argued an important case. Whatever it takes to get the job done, he always said. And a little deviousness was better than letting Kat do her stand-up act and mope while the Turnaround Formal and the proms just passed her by.

Still, Miranda worried. She tried to steady herself because it was Friday. She wanted to be together for Eric's game that night, and she needed her wits for the task ahead. Each Friday she had to deliver a class activity report for that week's issue of *Bay News*. Miranda didn't mind writing the report up, or using up her lunch period to deliver it. The problem was . . . editor Jackson Magruder.

Deciding that there was no way she was going to let Jackson get to her, Miranda strode into the main hallway, past the senior lockers and the trophy case where Eric's picture gazed back at her with confident eyes. Then she raced up the stairs, until she reached the journalism classroom. Steeling herself, she walked in.

"And now, it's time for today's interview," she heard Gabe croon over the newsroom's loudspeaker. She looked up, locating the speaker over the blackboard. While waiting to hear Kat's first big conversation with Brent Tucker, she slapped her briefcase on her lap and took out her class report.

Just go for it, Kat, Miranda prayed as she quickly proofed her report and the *Bay News* craziness buzzed around her. Fridays were always frantic. The *Bay News* staff had to get their final proof of the paper to a downtown printer by six. Kids were wailing on computers, and

Sarah Donovan was racing around the room with a sandwich and photos in hand. Jackson was bobbing from student to student, sticking his nose into everything, laughing and patting backs. Miranda glanced up. Jackson was having too good a time to even notice her.

When a silly array of sound effects marked the beginning of Brent's interview, Miranda listened carefully.

Kat's voice came out over the speaker. "Um, hi, Sea Lions," she began tentatively. "Today we're going to meet Bent Bruck . . . um, excuse me, I mean, Brent Tucker, a new junior who's just transferred here from . . . uh, um, where are you from, Brent?"

Miranda wanted to throw her briefcase across the room.

"San Rafael," Brent said. "Not too far from here."

"Oh. That's great," was all Kat could come back with. "San Francisco is . . . a great place." After that there was a pause. A long pause.

"Hey, did somebody turn off the radio show?" a senior yelled from the back of the newsroom.

Before anyone answered, Miranda heard Kat clear her throat, then let out a painfully awkward laugh. "Of course, you're not really from San Francisco, you're from San Rafael," Kat babbled. "That's what you said, isn't it?"

"That's right," Brent reacted.

After another horrendous space of dead air, Gabe jumped in with great energy. "So, Brent, what's it like to come from such a cool, big place like San Rafael, to a cool, little place like Crescent Bay?"

The show was back on track, but Kat had completely left the air. How could Kat be so witty and strong around her friends, then totally decompose around any guy she was attracted to? And Kat *was* attracted to Brent! Miranda had seen it the minute Kat had walked into the audio-visual room. Miranda felt a little sick as she listened to the next five minutes of the interview as Gabe and Brent chatted about rock music versus classical, which was apparently Brent's great love.

Just when Miranda didn't think she could listen anymore she caught something that made her perk up again. Brent was saying, "So anyway, I didn't want to make a big deal out of who my parents are, but I guess everyone knows anyway, so here goes. . . . "

The newroom noise softened. People glanced up.

"Okay. This is kind of embarrassing," Brent went on, "but I wanted to do something for the school. So I asked my dad to offer the use of our new ballroom. I know that the girl-ask-guy formal is coming up, and I know it has to be decided by whoever's in charge, but if you want to use our new Ocean Star Ballroom for the Turnaround dance, it's there to be used, free of charge."

Brent's announcement was followed by total silence. A moment later the room erupted with wild applause, whistles, and cheers.

"All right!" yelled a junior who tossed her typed pages into the air. "I couldn't face the gym for one more dance."

"Maybe I'll really ask someone now!" cried one of Jojo's fellow cheerleaders.

"YES!" Miranda cheered, jumping up, too. Maybe Brent wasn't the answer to Kat's dilemma, but he still might be the best thing that had ever happened to Cresent Bay High. As fast as she could, Miranda penned in Brent's offer on the bottom of her junior activity report. She considered just throwing her report on Mr. Weston's desk and not even looking at Jackson's handsome face.

But before she reached the desk, Jackson noticed her and feigned surprise. Yeah, I'm sure you're surprised, Miranda thought. She came in every Friday before they went to print. Jackson was probably as ready for her as she was for him. As he strolled over he tossed on his felt-brimmed hat and stuck his hands in the pockets of his vest. Then he swooped over to Sarah Donovan with a big smile and plucked an eight-by-ten photograph out of her hands. He waved it as he made his way over.

Miranda marched up to him first and held out her report. "Sorry the last part isn't typed," she said with clipped efficiency. "But I just added some important new information."

He took her report and traded her the photo. "What's this?"

"Something for the *National Enquirer*. Perfect teen couple have nine-headed baby. They make plans to form an entire baseball team and win a World Series."

It was the picture of Miranda and Eric taken on the football field, kissing with their arms around each other's necks. Couple of the Year. "You are so weird, Jackson."

He smiled proudly. "I know. Did you make any more decisions for our entire class today?"

Here we go, Miranda thought, telling herself to keep cool. Meanwhile every nerve in her body had zapped into red-hot alert. "Just look at this, okay? I don't like having to see you any more than you like having to see me."

"I never said that." Jackson looked over her typed pages. "This report is too long."

Miranda took a deep breath. "I just told you. We got some late news about the Tucker Resort and the Turnaround Formal. Brent Tucker is a junior. I wanted that news to be in my report."

"I can't promise it will all get printed."

"Why not? Can't you just make room for it?"

"I might." He gave her a flip smile. "But I also might need the extra room for another great photo or a last-minute news item."

"What last-minute item, Jackson? You go to print in five hours. What's going to happen in the next five hours?"

"Hey, you're the one who just added a last-minute entry. Maybe aliens will land."

"Please."

"Giant earthworms might take over the quad. You never know what's going to happen."

"Of course you do!" Miranda wanted to stuff

her report down his throat. "Look, Jackson, I
may not know exactly every little thing that's
going to happen but I can tell you what's happening right now. I'm trying to do my job, and
you're standing in my way. You have some kind
of thing against me, and I've had it."

He locked onto her with those green eyes
again. "What kind of thing?" he asked casually.

"I don't know what kind of thing. A thing.
A . . . a . . . thing!" Miranda couldn't believe
it. She tried to sound ultra calm, even though
she was gripping her briefcase so hard her knuckles were turning white. "I would appreciate it if
you would not go out of your way to make my
life difficult."

"Difficult!" His face took on a new seriousness, and his gaze took her in with fearless directness. "You think your life is difficult? Come
on, Miranda. You probably have it easier than
anyone I know."

She felt as if she'd just been hit with a rock.
"You don't know anything about me."

"So tell me what I need to know."

She looked at his face again and saw something
she didn't understand. It might have been a tiny
opening, or more likely it was the smug knowledge that he'd won another round. All she knew

was that he'd made her entire body charge up like she'd been facing a tidal wave, and she had no idea why Jackson even got to her. "I don't want to discuss this. I don't really want to talk to you anymore. All I want is to make sure that my class report will be properly printed in your newspaper. Is that too much to ask?"

When Jackson wouldn't give her an answer, Miranda clutched her briefcase and walked out.

After finishing her radio show, Kat's mind was on everything but her interview with Brent. She was thinking about finding a new best friend, going to look for Grady — the guy she'd met over the summer, dropping out of school, or just becoming a hermit and forgetting about guys for the rest of her life. Then thoughts of Brent came back, and she wondered how any boy could have eyes that blue. How big an idiot he must have thought she was after the way she'd bungled his interview!

"Bent Brucker. I still can't believe I called him that."

Cringing, she passed the science labs and headed up to the main building's second floor. Fifth period was starting in a few seconds, and the halls were emptying out. There were a few quick locker slams and teachers standing in their doorways waiting for the last of their students.

As soon as the show had ended, Kat had raced out of the radio station. There would be no comic monologue about this disaster. Because unlike Michael, Brent had gotten to her. Partly because he'd been so polite and decent and un-macho, but also because something about him made her blood feel like it had started flowing in the wrong direction. Even now Kat felt like she wanted to swim five thousand laps, hide under the covers, or throw herself down the stairs. Why couldn't she find a middle ground, like Miranda and Eric? She was either onstage, tongue-tied, or in over her head. No wonder she wanted to avoid the whole thing and stick with Gabe.

When she reached the second-floor landing, she tried to ignore the disappointment that still sat in the pit of her stomach. But then she took one last glance down the stairs and stopped breathing completely.

Brent was at the bottom of the stairway, hesitating over a campus map.

Kat let her bangs fall over her eyes and started for class.

"KAT!" Brent called out, before she'd taken two steps.

Kat's legs froze. Her heart double pumped.

Brent's loafers clacked as he quickly trotted up. Kat couldn't look at him, even though she could feel that he'd arrived on the landing and was standing only a few feet away.

"Where's room 118?" He was a little out of breath. "I forgot."

"That's the music room." She remembered him talking about how much he liked classical music. She liked classical music. "It's downstairs."

"Thanks."

She lifted her eyes a little, expecting that he'd be long gone. But he was still standing there. She wanted to apologize for putting him through that horrendous interview.

"Are you okay?" he asked before she could say anything.

"I'm fine."

A lock of golden hair fell over his left eye. "I just wanted to say thanks for letting me be on your show."

She almost laughed.

"Look, I haven't met very many people here

yet," he said quickly. "You know how weird it is being new. Anyway, you left so fast after the show was over. I just wanted you to know that I was really glad to meet you."

Kat stood there, hearing the kindness in his voice, but not believing that it could possibly be for real.

He took a slow step forward, and Kat felt her heart go into triple time. For a moment she didn't breathe or think or feel. All she did was watch his arm reach through the air until his hand touched her shoulder. It was a light touch, somewhere between a caress and a gentle tap.

"I mean it," he said. "I really hope to see you around." His blue eyes met hers. It wasn't until the bell rang that he finally turned and rushed back down the stairs.

Kat stood there breathing hard while the fifth-period bell screamed in her ears. She still felt Brent's hand on her shoulder. When she looked down, she almost expected to see a mark on her sleeve.

She suddenly felt as if her whole life had been turned upside down. She wanted to laugh, to weep, to turn cartwheels in the hall. Could it be that things might work out this time? Could this

be the time when she wasn't led on and dumped,
bored or boring, or giving a guy a bloody nose?
Was it possible that after the last half hour, she
was still someone that Brent Tucker wanted to
see around?

SEVEN

"Newspaper all done and ready to go for a ride."

At exactly five-nineteen that afternoon Jackson Magruder rolled up the final proof of *Bay News* and placed it in his backpack. He waited for Mr. Weston and the other staffers to say good-bye for the weekend, then slipped over to his locker, which was right outside the journalism room, and took out his skateboard.

Look right. Look left. All clear.

Jackson dropped the skateboard in the hallway, thumped it with the toe of his high-top, watched it somersault in front of him, and skillfully nabbed the board before it fell to the ground. It was a dumb kid trick he'd learned four years, five schools, and three towns ago. But he liked things that reminded him of freer times.

Closing his locker with his hip, Jackson

stepped onto his board, pushed off, and flew. After a week of putting together an issue of *Bay News*, the ride down to Gower's Print Shop was always filled with a delicious sense of satisfaction. Jackson loved the freedom of shooting down the hall like he was riding a big rapid. He threw his weight to one side and took a corner, his feet leaving the board for a moment as he crossed over the door frame and jumped outside. Riding the concrete pathways across the quad, he savored the ocean breeze and the way he felt the contours of the ground all the way up his legs. He even loved the risk and the thrill, since skateboards were strictly forbidden at Crescent Bay High.

Jackson crouched down as he glided over cracks in the sidewalk and dodged crumpled paper cups. Each Friday he took a different route off campus. This time he'd decided to swerve around the side of the gym, past the guidance office, and out onto Holiday Street, which would lead past a mini-mall and straight downtown. Jackson never wore a watch, but he knew that no matter what route he took, he should get to the printer with fifteen minutes to spare.

After almost losing his balance over a patch of bumpy grass, Jackson neared the gym. Campus energy was already focused on that night's football game. The Pep Club was hanging a huge spirit banner of a sea lion wearing a football helmet. The ticket takers were getting ready at the gate. Players were nervously arriving, and the cheerleaders were already dressed, practicing on the gym's front steps.

"GIVE ME A C," they rehearsed.

"GIVE ME AN R."

"R," Jackson repeated as he skated past the gym and away from the football madness. He figured that "R" would be his contribution toward the game that night. Not that he disliked football, but he wasn't as nuts about winning as the rest of the town seemed to be. Besides, it was too beautiful a night to be in a crowded stadium with a roof overhead. He'd rather spend it thinking, watching the sky shift while he skated up and down the beachfront promenade and waited to see how the night would unfold.

When he passed the guidance office, Jackson hopped off his skateboard and anchored it with his foot. He hadn't checked the activity board in days, so he looked it over in case there was news that might affect the newspaper. But before he checked any of the notices or lists, his hand went up, even though he wasn't quite sure what he was reaching for. He'd just seen a glimpse of his name on a folded piece of notebook paper that had been sealed with staples and taped to the glass-covered board.

At first Jackson assumed that the note had to do with the newspaper, although he wondered why it had been taped there, rather than handed to him in journalism class. He wondered why every corner had been stapled, as if he'd need a tool to open it. It wasn't until he pried the note off the board that he saw it had been taped over the Friends in Need announcements. He had to wonder if there was a connection.

"Probably not," he decided, taking in the orientation notice for the Friends in Need counselors.

The Friends in Need program had started about the time Jackson had moved to Crescent Bay. Even though he'd been new, he'd been chosen as a counselor because of the first piece he'd written for the paper, about a kid who went to a lot of different schools after his family had broken up. After last year's orientation, he'd gone to a weekend training session and a workshop over the summer. But as important as he'd found Friends in Need, no one had ever come to him for help.

Jackson stuck the note into his pocket and put one foot back on his skateboard. He remembered his six o'clock newspaper deadline and took one last survey of the whole board. But he ended up coming back to the Friends in Need notice again, reading the list of students who were to begin training the following week as new counselors.

"Come on," Jackson cried out loud. "Not Miranda. She can't be a new counselor. Give me a break."

Jackson would have marched right into the guidance office and asked, "Why Miranda?" except that he already knew the answer. Why not Miranda? She did everything else, so they probably threw in Friends in Need by default.

The more Jackson thought about Miranda's composed beautiful face, her stiff posture and decisive air, the more he wanted to shake some chaos into her. When he saw her lately, everything inside *him* went chaotic. He'd spent the first twelve years of his life being as sure and complacent as Miranda. And then, for the two years after his parents had split, he'd lived through four apartments and three of his mother's boyfriends. And when he saw how his mom had fallen apart, how completely unprepared she was for having the rug pulled out from under her, he knew that he could never let that happen to himself.

Jackson pushed off on his skateboard and thought about Miranda again. He couldn't stand one more exchange where nothing registered on her perfect face except the certainty that her life was all mapped out in front of her. He kept thinking about her as he scooted off campus and sped downtown. Miranda wanted to force everyone else into her rigid life plan. She wanted to storm straight ahead and pay no attention to the unexpected curves. Well, Jackson knew that life didn't follow plans. As soon as you tried to cram life into a square little box, it was all going to blow up in your face.

That night Miranda stared down at the oval football field. Eric and his teammates were warming up. Red-and-white uniforms were gathered in lines and clumps, some already marked with grass and dirt. She tried to locate Eric's number. She tried to remember Jojo's best cheers and who the tough players were on the Crowley High team. She'd never left school that afternoon. She'd stayed working on the car wash plans and tutoring a sophomore. Now the stadium bleachers were getting full, and the overhead lights stung Miranda's eyes.

"Eric's going to win again, Miranda. I can feel it," Miranda's father said. He sat next to her on the stadium bleachers in his three-piece suit and tie, holding a thermos, a program, and a pair of binoculars. "Any boy who's involved with my Miranda has to be a winner."

"I hope so." Miranda balanced her books on her lap and smiled.

"You hope so," Mr. Jamison teased. "What kind of attitude is that? You *know* so."

"I know so," she repeated.

"That's my girl."

Miranda nodded.

"It's too bad your mother couldn't make it tonight," her dad added, clapping his hands and watching the field. "But she had to go right back for that real estate conference. She just may get that deal for Hunter's Bluff."

"I understand," Miranda said, swallowing her disappointment. Miranda's mom developed real estate, and the recent boom in Crescent Bay had made her incredibly, successfully busy. Lately Miranda didn't see her for whole days at a time. Despite his own super busy schedule, her dad had been trying to pick up the slack. Miranda was just getting used to spending more time with him. "Thanks for skipping your business dinner so you could come, Dad. I really appreciate it."

"I wouldn't miss this." He grinned and put his arm around Miranda, planting a kiss on her temple. "I wouldn't miss it for your sake, or for Eric's. Two more wins and Eric goes to district play-offs."

Miranda glanced back briefly at Kat and Jojo who sat one bleacher up, jabbering to each other and saving seats for Chip and Gabe. Miranda hadn't talked to Kat since lunch. She still felt guilty over having pushed Brent on her. She wanted to ignore her father and yell, "Kat, I'm sorry! I won't do it again." At the same time, the argument with Jackson echoed in her brain. But her father accepted no excuses for acting wimpy or whiny, so she sat up very straight and stared back down at the field.

Mr. Jamison flipped through the athletic program and looked at Eric's stats. "We'll leave first thing tomorrow morning to drive to Stanford," he announced.

That was another thing making Miranda feel unsteady. Her father had suddenly decided that she and Eric had to visit his old law school alma mater. Probably the best university on the West Coast, Stanford was a two-hour drive from Crescent Bay. Eric thought it was a great idea, but Miranda had a million things to do, and they would be gone for the entire Saturday.

"I called a friend of mine who's a law professor there, and he wants to meet you and Eric."

"Why?"

"Why do you think?" her father answered, closing his program and setting it on the bench. "Trust me on this one. It's for your own good. When you finish law school, you'll thank me." He squeezed her shoulder and stood up. "Well, I didn't have time for dinner, as usual, so I guess I'll go grab a hamburger." He finally turned back to acknowledge Kat and Jojo. "Anybody want anything to munch on?"

Jojo put her hand to her cheerleading sweater. "I can't cheer on a full stomach."

"I had an early dinner at home," said Kat.

"Miranda?"

"No, thanks. I'm not hungry."

"Of course you are," her father responded in a robust voice. "Now put your books away for the next few hours. There's a time to work and a time to play. Relax and enjoy yourself. Eric's going to win!" He tousled her hair, then trotted down to the snack bar.

After he was gone, Miranda finally turned all the way around and looked up at Kat and Jojo. "Enjoy myself," she scoffed. She waited for an angry look in Kat's eyes, but saw nothing but her best friend's usual warmth and humor. "It's a little hard to enjoy myself, considering that I have a monster chem test next week and a meeting every single day. Plus I'm supposed to have everything ready for the car wash by Monday."

"DON'T HAVE A BREAKDOWN!" Kat and Jojo said at the same time.

"What can we do to help?" Jojo offered, massaging Miranda's shoulders.

Kat leaned her head against Miranda's other arm. "I'll come over on Sunday and help you with the car wash stuff as soon as I'm done working on the show with Gabe."

"You will?" Miranda couldn't believe that Kat had forgiven her so easily. Actually, everything about Kat looked amazingly relaxed and cheerful, from her crisp walking shorts to her sweater with prancing reindeer. She'd even changed the things hanging from her necklace. Now there was a bubble wand, a little stuffed anteater, and a red-and-white spirit streamer. "Kat, you're in such a good mood."

Kat threw her program into the air and kept laughing.

Miranda breathed a sigh of relief. "I was worried that after that interview today, you'd be mad at me. I'm sorry."

"She *was* mad at you," Jojo interrupted. Kat shushed her, but Jojo went right on. "Kat and I talked this whole thing over between fifth and sixth periods. Kat *was* mad at you. But she isn't anymore. Now she adores you as only a best friend can."

"Gee, thanks, Jojo," Kat said, tugging at the pompom on Jojo's aerobic shoe. "Next time I need an interpreter, I'll call on you."

"What happened?" Miranda asked Kat. "I know why you *were* mad, and I deserved it. How come you're not mad anymore?"

"She wouldn't tell me that," Jojo confessed.

"It's a secret," Kat teased, tugging Miranda's hair. "I might tell you by the time of the Turnaround Formal. But then again, I might not. And unlike Jojo, I can keep a secret."

"Did you ask someone to the dance?" Miranda gasped. Had Kat fallen for someone else after the disaster with Brent?

"No." Kat gave Miranda a coy smile. "Not yet."

"Kat!" Miranda cried. "Are you going to ask someone? Who? Can you double with me and Eric?"

Kat just gave a coy smile. "Wait and see."

Jojo assured Miranda, "I'll find out who it is. No one has been able to avoid my methods so far."

"Try me." Kat swept her hand across her mouth, as if she were closing a zipper. Then Jojo grabbed her, and Miranda began tickling Jojo. Pretty soon all three of them were sputtering and laughing.

When Miranda's father reappeared, stopping on the edge of the field to chat with Eric, Jojo jumped up and straightened her red-and-white skirt. "I'd better run to my locker and get you that car wash flier before the game starts. I remembered to make it for you in my computer class, but I forgot to bring it."

"Are you sure you have time?" Kat asked. "I can get it."

Jojo patted the bench. "You stay here or you'll lose Chip's and Gabe's seats. The game won't start for another fifteen minutes. I have time."

Before Kat and Miranda could stop her, Jojo

was already wiggling around knees and stepping over people's feet, until she reached the end of the bleacher and jumped down. The crowd was getting thick now, and the overhead lights had been turned on. Jojo was actually glad to get away for a few minutes and collect herself before the game. Sometimes she felt like odd man out around Miranda and Kat. Miranda was brilliant, and Kat was funny. What was she? Just nice clothes, a pretty face, a chatty mouth, and a toothpaste smile.

She jogged away from the stadium, against the flow of traffic, past the snack bar and the ticket takers, through the parking lot that was filled with cars and people and buses from the opposing school. As quick as she was graceful, she leaped over a bench, passed the guidance office, and quickly found herself in the dusky quad. A few people were taking shortcuts across the grass, but once Jojo got to the outdoor library hallway, the crowd seemed to disappear.

Jojo stopped for a moment when she heard the band begin their warmup. Leaning over for a stretch, she caught her reflection in the library window. Sometimes she had to look in the mirror to make sure that she existed. Buying clothes was the same way. So was gossiping. As long as she had great dirt to spread, everyone would always need to talk to her.

She stared in the window and tried to think about the game. Watching herself, she did a leap, taking careful notice of how her back arched. She practiced her touchdown smile. She turned to the side and kicked, staring hard again to check the height and straightness of her leg until she heard a sound and quickly turned.

"Is someone there?" Jojo asked sharply, looking down toward her locker.

Someone *was* there, Jojo realized as her heart jumped up in her chest. And that someone had been there the whole time that Jojo was prancing around staring at herself. Jojo was too embarrassed to stare, but she'd already caught a glimmer of pale, almost white hair. If it weren't for her loyalty to Miranda, she would have turned around and run back to the field.

Jojo stepped toward her locker. As she got closer, the girl turned, then started to walk away. That's when Jojo recognized Leanne Heard. Jojo's embarrassment turned to anger as she sensed that Leanne was acting weird . . . or rather, weirder than usual. It was as if Leanne were embarrassed, too, as if she'd also been caught doing something she didn't want other people to see.

"Hey," Jojo called out.

Leanne stopped, then turned around and walked back with a few defiant strides. She had her hands in the pockets of a huge dark coat, like something made for an old-fashioned army winter. Leanne's hair, usually striking in its lush unnatural blondness, looked a little stringy.

Jojo stepped closer, too, until she and Leanne were only a few feet apart. Between them were their two gray locker doors. Out of some unstoppable social reflex, Jojo smiled.

Leanne just stared.

Even though Leanne was strange, even spooky, Jojo couldn't stand the fact that Leanne never returned her smiles. They sat next to one another in English. Jojo would be chatting and smiling at everyone before class, while Leanne looked right through her. In spite of all the other people waving and saying hello, Leanne could make her feel invisible.

"Are you going to the game?" Jojo asked. As soon as the words were out of her mouth, she saw Leanne's dark red mouth lift in a smirk. Jojo wished she could grab her words out of the air and swallow them back down again.

"Oh, yes," Leanne said sarcastically. Her voice was husky, like a rock singer who'd been screaming her guts out. "But I left my pompoms at home. Is that a criminal offense? Maybe you'll have to tell everyone in our English class about it."

"Why would I do that?"

Leanne glanced at her locker. She still seemed oddly nervous. "Why would you come back here when there's a game going on? What are you trying to do, look in my locker so you can tell everyone about me?"

"Why would I want to look in your locker? And the game hasn't started."

When Leanne didn't answer, Jojo had to wonder if she hadn't hit a nerve. Maybe that was why Leanne was acting especially bizarre. Maybe she had caught Leanne trying to break into *her* locker. Jojo tried to remember what she had worth stealing and thought of her car wash flier and her private notes about the Turnaround dance.

"How do I know you weren't going through *my* locker?" Jojo accused.

Leanne folded her arms and let out a hoarse laugh. "That's great. Finally you drop that phony smile of yours and say what you really think."

"What?"

"You really think I'm a thief, and that I'm not good enough to share a hallway with you and your friends. At least you finally admit it now. And I'm sure you'll tell everyone else in school."

"I will not!"

"Yes, you will," Leanne spat out. She started to go, then turned back. "You won't be able to help yourself."

EIGHT

"G₀ . . . Go . . . Go . . . GO . . . GO!!!!
GOOOOOOOO SEEEEE LIIIII-YUUUNS!"

There was less than a minute left in the game's second quarter, but Crescent Bay High was behind, 0–6. Despite Jojo's near hysterical cheering, it didn't look like much was going to happen before halftime. The Sea Lions were looking at their first loss of the season.

"Wait just a minute, Chip!" Gabe cried as he and Chip turned by the edge of the field. They'd left the bleachers early but spun back to stare as their quarterback suddenly pitched the ball three quarters of the way across the field. It was heading right to Eric, who was running toward the end zone with his arms outstretched.

"LET'S TURN THIS GAME AROUND!" Chip screamed. "YES! Catch it, Geraci. CATCH IT!"

Eric knocked into one tackle and swerved away from another until he was clear and the football sailed into his hands. Another two steps and it was 6–6. Eric threw down the football and thrust his fists into the air.

The crowd went crazy.

"ALL RIGHT, MAN!" Chip screamed.

"YAAAAHOOOOOOOOOOOEEE!" Gabe cheered.

"Amazing," Chip sighed, after the noise had died down and the Crescent Bay team was lining up for the kick.

"Yup."

"Eric Geraci." Chip shook his head, and his long hair swayed. "That guy is so smooth. If that had been me, I would have asked the tackle if he minded getting out of my way."

Gabe laughed. "So Eric Geraci can catch a football. There are other things in life."

"I know."

They watched the successful kick and heard the cheering explode again. 7–6. Crescent Bay High was headed for yet another win.

"You are about to be smooth, too," Gabe said with a mischievous grin. "Come on. No more stalling." He led Chip to the back of the bleachers where a lot of kids collected during halftime.

It was crowded, and they had to avoid three different girls who hung off the bleachers to flirt with Gabe. The marching band was lining up for the halftime show, waiting to file through the tunnel that led onto the field.

"Is she still there?" Chip said, stepping onto the soccer field, his back to the snack bar. He stamped his sandals, trying to get warm. His mouth had become very dry.

Gabe craned his neck. "Lisa Avery is still there. For once she's alone, too. She's getting in line at the snack bar. If you're sure you want to go through with this, the moment is now."

Chip's courage began to crumble. "Maybe Jojo *was* just joking about my being on that list. What makes you think I can get Lisa to ask me to the Turnaround dance?"

Gabe shrugged. "She's probably going to ask somebody. Why shouldn't it be you?"

"I can give you about a hundred and ten reasons." Chip moved in front of some little kids playing with a Crescent Bay High pennant and located Lisa. Her back was to him but he saw her flaming red hair and astonishing body in a short, tight skirt and form-fitting sweater. He looked for her infamous little gold anklet, which was engraved with the name of whatever guy she supposedly liked that week. But Chip was too far away to see anything but shifting shoulders and brilliantly colored hair. "So you've already been asked to the Turnaround Formal, right?"

"Twice," Gabe said. "Shelley Lara and Amy Zandarski. I told them both no. I'm going alone. The dance committee asked me to do the music."

"Wait a minute," Chip objected. "How come you're giving me advice when you're going to the dance alone?"

Gabe faced him, and for a moment Chip thought he was going to respond as one of his radio characters. But Gabe answered straight. "I don't really want to go with somebody, I guess. I'd rather flirt at school and goof around with Kat, but that's only because Kat and I are just friends." He shook his head and looked off. "But I'm talking about me, not you. Don't let Lisa scare you. She's just a girl."

"That's like saying the Beatles were just a rock group."

Gabe laughed. "Just go up to Lisa and say hi. Make small talk, crack a few jokes, then ask — very casually — if she's invited anyone to the Turnaround dance. If she says yes, then shake your head like she really missed out on something and walk away. I'm telling you, she'll be intrigued."

"What if she says no, she hasn't asked anybody yet?"

"Then slip her your phone number."

"Slip her my phone number!"

Gabe snapped his finger and pointed. "Write it on the palm of her hand and look in her eyes while you do it."

Chip could picture Gabe pulling off a move like that. But if *he* did it, he'd probably worry about toxic ink on the girl's skin or whether his pen point might puncture her. "Write it on her hand. How do you think of these things?"

"The important thing is to stay loose," Gabe instructed. "Don't lose your cool. Don't lose your sense of humor."

"I feel like I'm going to throw up," Chip admitted. "Is this how girls feel when they're trying to get asked to big dances?" He shook his head and tried to walk away. "I should just drop hints to some freshman in the Environmentalists. Or I should stay home the night of the dance and save gasoline. Why am I doing this?"

"You told me you wanted to do this!" Gabe

grabbed his shoulders. "You're doing it because you have the hots for Lisa."

"But so does every other guy in this school. She probably doesn't know who I am after all. And from what I've heard she just chews guys up and throws them away."

"CHIP! Who you're attracted to and who your brain says is the right person aren't usually the same. If they were, all our lives would be a lot simpler." Gabe pushed him another few feet closer to the snack bar. "Go, Chip. She's at the order window. Go."

Chip took one step, then looked back like a kid going away to camp.

"GO."

Chip nodded and went. "Go, Chip," he said to himself as he shuffled through the crowd. "Excuse me," he said to an old lady. "Sorry. Oops. Can I please get through?" He passed Jojo, who was leaping off in the other direction, smiling and waving her red-and-white glove. He listened to the marching band. He thought about how he'd never go out for football because he was too thin, and how the idea of slamming into another human made him sick to his stomach.

But before Chip could think or worry anymore, he was there. The back of Lisa's red hair was practically tickling his nose as she chatted with some older-looking guy who was still in line. She'd already bought her snacks, some soda and red licorice. Chip watched as she giggled, posed, and sighed. Her perfume even overpowered the smell of chili and burgers.

Finally she turned to head back to the bleachers. Chip tried to move out of her way and get her attention at the same time, but all he succeeded in doing was slamming into her, then grabbing her right around the rib cage.

"Sorry!"

"Look out," she cried as she started to drop her snack box.

Chip grabbed it out of her hands. His face was hot, and he couldn't think. The top of the paper cup had popped off and soda was running down his arm. "My fault."

"You bet it is."

"Here, let me buy you another soda," he said, trying to hold the box and dig in his pocket for change.

She grabbed the box back from him. "You don't have to buy me another one. Just look where you're going."

"I'm really sorry."

She tossed back that incredible-colored hair

and started back toward the bleachers. Chip stayed by her side, noticing that she wore pink lip gloss that looked like she'd just been eating gooey mints. Her eyes were rimmed with smoky makeup that gave her a sultry, heavy-lidded look.

Chip kept pace with her for another ten feet. He wanted to go back to Kat and Miranda, but he couldn't go back to Gabe without at least giving this a decent try. "Man, you know that stuff is full of chemicals," he finally said, pointing to her soda.

"Really?" Lisa answered in mock surprise. "And I thought diet sodas grew on trees." Then she just stood there, looking into his eyes with her famous sultry expression. When guys talked about her — and they did endlessly — it was that expression they remembered even more than her flirting or her body. But Chip didn't take in the sexiness in her eyes. He was too struck by the clear message that she didn't know who he was.

"Didn't we meet at the . . . recycling rally?" Chip asked desperately. He felt like he was doing one of Kat and Gabe's routines, except that no one was laughing.

"I don't think so."

"My name is Chip. I know we've met before . . . somewhere."

"If you say so."

This was hopeless. Chip just decided to go for broke and then make a quick getaway. "So . . . have you asked anybody to the Turnaround Formal yet?"

She let her head fall back and she laughed, a lusty laugh that seemed to come from the tips of her toes. "Is that what this is about?" She patted him on the top of the head. "Oh, Chip," she pouted. "You said your name was Chip, right?"

He nodded.

"What's that short for? Chipper?"

Chip wanted to crawl under the bleachers. "Charles actually."

"Well, Charles, you're very sweet."

"Gee, thanks."

She kissed her finger, then placed her finger on his lips. "No, I haven't asked anyone to the Turnaround dance yet," she said with condescending sultriness. "But when I do ask someone, you can bet I'll give you very serious consideration."

Chip nodded while she giggled at him, then turned and flounced away.

"Thanks a lot, Gabe," Chip grumbled. He was no longer cold. In fact, he was sweating, but still feeling sick. He remembered Jojo saying that he might be better off not knowing Lisa. Well, Jojo was right, he realized. As far as Chip was concerned, it was better to be overlooked, than to get pounced on by a girl like Lisa.

They won.

After the game was over, when Eric had showered and dressed and was heading out to meet Miranda, two words were still going off like flashbulbs in his head. WE WON. I WON. Another win the following week and they would go to district.

"Great game, Geraci," said Alex Corley, the first-string quarterback.

"You, too, man," Eric answered as they walked out of the gym together carrying their bags and wearing proud grins. "That pass was perfect, Alex. Perfect."

"Your receiving was perfect, too," Alex swore. He stopped on the gym steps, just under the Sea Lion banner. "Look who's waiting for you," he said, pointed to Miranda who stood with her father.

"Yeah," Eric said, waiting a moment and staring, as if he were freeze-framing the entire evening. It was all so perfect that he never wanted any bit of it to change. Miranda's long, dark hair glistened under the lights. Her posture was upright and strong as she stood with her hands in her pockets, scuffing her boot back and forth across the ground. And next to her was Mr. Jamison, carrying her briefcase and checking his watch.

Eric bolted down the gym steps and threw his arms around Miranda. She had some papers under one arm, but she still lifted her delicate face to kiss him. Eric laughed as his wet hair dribbled onto her forehead, one drop running down the bridge of her nose. He kissed the drop, then turned back to see if the other guys on the team were watching.

"Congratulations, son," said Mr. Jamison, adding a strong handshake. "Great game. You should be proud."

Eric was proud.

"You were great," Miranda added. "The second quarter was so exciting."

"Thanks." He pulled back a little to look at her face again. In spite of her beauty, she looked a little tired.

"Everybody went ahead to the Wave," she

told him. "I guess we can meet them there. They can't wait to see you and tell you how great you were."

"Wait a minute," Mr. Jamison interrupted. He grinned and began to lead them toward the parking lot. "How about if I take you two out someplace really nice first to celebrate? I mean someplace really first class. Not that I want to keep you away from your friends, but I think a very special celebration is in order."

"Great!" Eric exclaimed. He loved the idea of walking into one of the exclusive tourist restaurants with Miranda on his arm and a winning smile on his face. He turned to check with Miranda, but she was looking down at her hands. He got that sense, sometimes, that she was trying to pull in the opposite direction from him. He suddenly felt as if he were dragging her along the blacktop.

"Miranda?" Eric prodded.

She shrugged and stopped completely. Then she leaned in, grabbed the hem of Eric's jean jacket, and said in a soft voice, "Everyone is waiting for us at the Wave. I want to see Kat. And we have to leave really early tomorrow to go to Stanford. I have a ton of stuff to do."

Eric saw the strain around her blue eyes, but

he ignored it. He wanted to skip his special celebration about as much as he wanted to go back to the end of the second quarter and drop that ball.

"Come on," he teased, slinging his arm around her again and actually picking her up off the ground. "We'll go out with your dad, and then we can meet everybody at the Wave. If I know Gabe and Jojo, they'll be there until at least one. We can sleep in the car tomorrow on the way to Stanford." He looked to Mr. Jamison for approval.

Mr. Jamison got on Miranda's other side and the two of them playfully escorted her across the parking lot.

"Eric's right," Mr. Jamison argued. "Sleep when you can. When you have your own law practice, you'll have to work all day, play all night, and then go back the next morning and kill them in court."

Miranda looked back and forth from Eric to her father. Finally she folded against Eric. "Okay," she sighed. "Let's go."

NINE

"Leanne?"

When Leanne heard the voice, she made herself wait for a moment, so as not to seem too eager or too desperate. She was sitting on a bench where the beachfront promenade met busy Ocean Avenue. Gulls flapped and waves rumbled. The Tucker Resort towered behind her, with its outdoor elevator gliding up and down like a giant glass zipper on the cliff. It was noon on Saturday, and tourists were riding rented pedal cars in the direction of the old amusement park.

"Leanne?" he repeated.

Leanne shoved her hands into the pockets of the fur jacket she'd found at a thrift store, a jacket she hadn't worn to school since girls had made comments about it having fleas. She could just imagine what those girls would say if they saw the inside of her locker.

"You are Leanne Heard, aren't you?"

Finally Leanne looked up. "That's me." Jackson Magruder was standing next to her, wearing two sweatshirts layered on top of one another, jeans, and a wool vest.

He sat down and placed his skateboard on his lap. "Great day," he said, breathing in the ocean air as if he were testing it. His cheeks were flushed, and there was a trace of sweat on his upper lip. "Am I late? The way the light was coming through the clouds was really amazing. I stopped for a while to look." He wiped his forehead with his sleeve. "Totally great day."

"Yeah." Leanne hadn't noticed. "You showed up."

"I got your note on the activity board," Jackson answered simply. He brushed sand off one hand. "Why wouldn't I show up?"

"You don't exactly know me." She dug her hands into her pockets again and looked around to make sure that no one from school was strolling by. "You know, I just left that note for you because your name was on the list of that peer group at school, that, what's it called, peer helper thing?"

"Friends in Need."

Leanne cringed as the wind plastered a strand of platinum hair across her mouth. "Dumb name."

Jackson spun one of the wheels on his skateboard. "Why did you want to talk to me?"

Leanne wasn't really sure, except that she had to talk to someone. From what she'd seen of Jackson, she didn't think he'd blab, or try and put the moves on her. And she thought he'd understand something besides absurd pep rallies and having a dance at the Tucker Resort.

"I liked it when you got up at the quad assembly," she admitted. "At least you have the nerve to try and shake things up a little. I thought that was fairly cool."

"Thanks." He smiled. "Shaking things up is what it's all about."

"Yeah. Especially when it comes to the smile crowd."

"Who?"

"Joanne Hernandez and her gang."

"Oh."

"I'm sure there are phonier people in our class," Leanne justified. "I just don't have to have my locker next to them."

Jackson nodded.

Leanne stood up. "Hey, can we walk or something? I feel kind of weird just sitting around here." She stamped her feet, and her secondhand high heels clacked against the sandy concrete.

"Sure. Where do you want to go?" He tucked his skateboard under his arm and waited for her to pick the direction. She led him away from the far-off rumble of the roller coaster and toward the Tucker Resort, past the old hotels and in front of the biggest, fanciest houses that looked out over the water.

Jackson dropped his skateboard on the promenade, then rode alongside her. He leaned his head back, as if the air were caressing his face. For a while, neither of them spoke. Soon they were leaving the big houses behind and passing the entrance to the Crescent Bay Aquarium, which was decorated with flags and paintings of fish. When they finally neared the big new parking lot that was below the Tucker Resort, Leanne left the promenade and headed away from the resort onto the sand.

She took off her shoes as Jackson hopped off his skateboard and scooped it up. They jogged all the way down to the water's edge.

"My homeroom teacher told us about the Friends in Need deal," Leanne said, kicking aside driftwood and clumps of seaweed. "He said I could talk to you and you wouldn't tell anyone. Is that right?"

"That's right."

"Okay. I just need some advice about something. It's no huge deal."

Jackson skipped a rock. "We're not actually supposed to even give advice. At the training sessions they told us just to listen and see if we could help, but not to talk too much."

"Great," Leanne said. "If I needed someone to stand there like a post, I could have stayed home with my mother."

He smiled.

"Of course, if I wanted to hear somebody talk all the time and not say anything," she ranted, "I could have stuck around with my mother's boyfriend."

"I remember those."

"Those what?"

"Mother's boyfriends. My mom went through some real losers."

Leanne took a deep breath and began to relax. Not that Jackson was going to be the answer to her problem, or someone she'd even talk to again, but she was glad that for once in her life,

she'd opened up to someone. "What happened?
With your mom, I mean?"

"She got married again just before we moved
here." Jackson wrapped his arms around himself
as a breeze came up and ruffled his spiky hair.
"My stepdad's okay. He's a good guy. But I still
don't quite trust it. Things were crazy after my
mom and dad broke up, so I figure that things
could get crazy again. You always have to be
prepared."

"Yeah, my life is pretty crazy, too. Especially
since my mom's boyfriend moved in." Leanne
took a deep breath and watched the waves.
"Maybe it would be less crazy if he left. Then
maybe I could move back home." She dropped
her bomb casually, then waited for a reaction.

Sure enough Jackson froze, not moving even
when the water rushed up and soaked his shoes.

She finally looked right at him. There was an
intensity in his eyes that almost made her take a
step back.

"You're not living at home?" he asked.

"No way."

"Where are you living?"

"In a pretty nice place near downtown," she
lied. She *was* living near downtown, but her

rooming house was anything but nice. There
was just a bed, a dresser, and a sink, with a toilet
down the hall. Half the time there was no hot
water, which was why she'd been sneaking
showers at school and keeping everything —
shampoo, clothes, towels, hair color — in her
locker. "It's okay."

"Really?"

"Anyway," she blurted out, wondering how
long she could keep Jojo from seeing the inside
of her locker, and how fast the word would
spread if Jojo ever did see that it was practically
a motel closet. "What I need is advice about
finding a job. I have to pay for everything now,
and I spent all the money I had."

"What about all the tourist places?"

She wrapped her jacket collar around her chin.
She'd really wanted advice about more than just
a job, but it was too strange and scary to go any
further out on a limb. "I did the want ad thing,
but I didn't find anything."

He turned around and looked back at the cliffs.
"What about the Tucker Resort? I saw something in the paper that said they're hiring tons
of people."

"Right," she scoffed. She hadn't wanted to
admit that the tourist shops took one look at her

and tucked their HELP WANTED signs under the counters. She could just imagine what they would think at the swank new Tucker Resort.

"Why not?" He shrugged. "You should just go up there and talk to them. If you don't try stuff now, you'll just get thrown into things and you won't know how to handle it." He kicked some wet sand. "Shoot. I'm giving advice, which I'm not supposed to do. Still, I think checking out the Resort is worth a try."

Leanne turned around and watched the zipper elevator again. Up and down it crawled. Up and down.

They stood on the sand a while longer until Leanne couldn't risk standing there anymore. She'd taken a big enough chance by leaving Jackson that note. Sure, he hadn't laughed at her, and he hadn't made a move. But he still ran the school newspaper. He was involved and respected and all that. Maybe his parents had been divorced, but that didn't mean he'd ever seen things through her eyes.

She led the way back to the promenade, then shrugged. "Look, I really appreciate you meeting me and talking to me and all, but I can take it from here."

He looked surprised. "You sure? I don't feel

like I really helped you very much."

She looked up at the Resort again. What a weird town, she thought, where she lived in a room with no hot water, while filthy rich tourists used their American Express cards to play golf and drink champagne. "I'm okay."

He put his skateboard down. "Maybe I'll see you around school. If you want to talk or anything, just leave a note for me again. And if you want to talk to some professional-type person, I have a list of names at home."

"Yeah. See you. Thanks and all."

Jackson watched her with a concerned expression until she slipped her shoes back on and ran across the prom. She quickly left Jackson behind and turned into the Tucker Resort parking lot, weaving around the Mercedes and the Cadillacs. She wrote her initials on the dusty window of a BMW, and then she stopped to look up at the outdoor elevator again.

Why not? she asked herself. One thing that living on her own had taught her was a certain nerviness about the real world. At school she felt like she was underwater, but on weekends downtown, she knew the territory like the back of her hand.

She made her way to an entrance with an awning and ignored the doorman. After pushing her way through a revolving door, she stopped for a moment. The lobby was odorless and cool. There were huge potted trees and deep green carpets, wicker furniture and a string quartet playing lively music in one corner. Middle-aged people in expensive, casual clothes strolled leisurely while uniformed employees bustled about. The whole thing was so lush and ritzy that Leanne almost burst out laughing.

Sticking her hands into her pockets, Leanne strutted through the lobby, as if she were wearing a designer fur, rather that a moth-eaten hand-me-down. She didn't dare speak to anyone, but found a directory that showed an employment office on the second floor. She passed a big window that looked out over tennis courts and a sign that read OCEAN STAR BALLROOM. But it wasn't until she found the elevator that she allowed herself to look up and take in another face.

And that was when she saw him, just before she pressed the elevator button. He appeared from out on the tennis courts and was walking quickly toward her, wearing a pressed long-sleeve shirt over plaid shorts, and tennis shoes with no socks. She stared because he was so handsome. And because she recognized him from school and was trying to remember why. Then it hit her. She'd overheard Jojo going on about him in English class, and she'd seen him once after school when he was getting into an expensive car with a personalized license plate. Brent Tucker.

Brent completely passed her by, then stopped.

Leanne pressed the button for the elevator.

He turned slowly as if he'd seen her through his back. He stared and smiled and took two steps closer. "Do I know you?"

"Where do I go to apply for a job?" she asked, avoiding his question and his curious eyes.

"Get off on the second floor and go right." He stuck his hands in his pockets and continued to stare. One corner of his mouth lifted in a little smile. "You can't miss it."

She nodded and looked back at the elevator lights, hoping that the doors would open soon. A second later, the bell pinged and the elevator arrived. But the doors didn't open right away. She wanted to pry them open with her fingers.

Brent took another big step toward her. "I'll go with you. Why don't I show you how to get there?"

But before he could reach her, the doors finally did slide open, and Leanne slipped in. She furiously punched the second-floor button, and the doors snapped closed.

As the elevator climbed, and Leanne looked out the glass at the curving coastline, she thought about Brent Tucker. She still saw his smile and felt his lingering stare.

TEN

"KAAAT! GABE'S HERE," Kat's mother yelled up from the first floor of their rambling Victorian.

Kat put her hand over her phone receiver, pounded her bedroom floor, and yelled down, "SEND HIM UP. I'M TALKING TO MIRANDA."

"Anyway," Kat said, going back to the phone, "Jojo called me first thing yesterday and went on and on about it." She heard Gabe stop at the foot of the stairs to joke with a pair of tourists from LA. Kat's folks had turned their big, old house into a bed and breakfast, with the first floor set up for guests and the family's private rooms upstairs. Kat's bedroom was small with a slanted ceiling, one big window, mattress on the floor, desk, a picture of Lily Tomlin and one of Janet Evans, plus Kat's usual mess, which included half-read novels and unfinished homework.

"Jojo really said that Leanne Heard was trying to break into her locker Friday night?" Miranda asked.

"That's what she said — among other things, like who's on her possible Turnaround dance list now, and which cheerleader is cheating on her boyfriend. I couldn't follow it all."

"Leanne Heard," Miranda considered. "Didn't she go to middle school with us? I can barely remember her."

Kat walked her bare feet up the wallpaper. She'd left her swimsuit under her shorts and sweater, and it was still a little damp from that morning's workout. "Leanne grew up here, just like we did. I was in a class with her freshman year. I kind of liked her, even though a lot of people think she's weird. Of course, a lot of people think I'm weird." Gabe knocked. "ENTERRR."

Gabe wandered in and plopped down on her bed.

"Gabe just landed," Kat told Miranda.

Gabe waved, then began looking through Kat's books, as if it were his room. He found a cookie tin filled with music tapes that Kat's dad had left for her.

Kat watched him. "How's your mom?" she asked Miranda.

"She's sleeping."

"Oh. How was going to visit Stanford yesterday with Eric and your dad?"

"Okay. Dad and Eric talked about practicing law the whole time. I guess Eric's thinking about becoming a lawyer now."

"Really? Somehow I can't see Eric as a lawyer. Can you?"

When Miranda didn't respond, Kat looked at Gabe again. He had plucked an opera tape out of the cookie tin and was making a face at it. Kat stuck out her tongue. "Miranda, I'd better go before Gabe ruins all my stuff. It's like having another brother. If I didn't watch him, he'd rip the heads off my old dolls."

Gabe gave her a fiendish look.

Kat went back to Miranda. "I'll come over and help with the car wash stuff when Gabe and I are done working on our show. You sure you're okay?"

"I'm fine. Bring your algebra book when you come, and I'll help you study."

"Great."

"See you soon."

Kat hung up. Then she watched Gabe again and smiled. He was in his normal high-tops, black T-shirt, and jeans, with his normal curly hair and funny, hyper air. And yet everything about him looked even warmer and more fun than usual. Kat smiled. She was still feeling like she could leap up and kiss the sky.

"You never told me you used to play with dolls," Gabe said. "I always assumed you were into GI Joe."

Kat threw a pillow at him.

He caught it and put it under his head. Lying on his back, he went through her tapes again. "So where'd you get these classical tunes all of a sudden? Puccini. Brahms. Oh, here's a good one. Gregorian chants. Try dancing to that one."

"I borrowed them from my dad." She lunged over and tried to grab the tin away. "Gabe, do you always have to go through my stuff?"

Gabe played keep away with the tin, then flew across the bed, took hold of her arm, and began to wrestle. He locked one leg over hers and grabbed for her middle.

"Gabe!" Kat gasped, pulling down the hem of her sweater and kicking. "NO! Don't! Please! GABE!"

Gabe was laughing, too, but he wouldn't let up. "Tell me the truth," he teased, pinning down her hands. "Why this sudden interest in classical music?"

"I just wanted to listen!" she managed to say as she kicked and squirmed. "Let me go!"

"Not until you tell me what's going on. Why the sudden interest in old people's music?"

"It's not old people's music. And who says I'm suddenly interested? GABE! LET ME UP!" She pushed against him with all her strength, finally throwing him back onto the mattress and freeing herself. They both sat up and looked at each other.

After a pause, Gabe held up the cookie tin and shook it with a suspicious smile.

Kat plucked the tin out of his hands. "Let's just work on our next show," she begged. Then she lightly bopped his head with the tin and tossed it under her desk.

Gabe rubbed his head. "Ouch. Okay." He took a little pad of paper out of his back pocket and flipped it open.

"Good," Kat crawled across the floor, found her notebook, and took a pen out of her zippered, plastic sack. "We need a topic."

"Topic . . . topic." Gabe sat back against the

wall and closed his eyes. "Essay tests. The beach. White mice in science class. Quad project."

"We've done all those."

"Computers. Girls' B ball. Parents. Showers in gym class. Tucker Resort."

"What?" Kat felt her heart lurch.

"The Tucker Resort." Gabe opened his eyes and frowned. "You don't want to do a routine about that, do you?"

"No," she blurted out. "Keep going."

He stared at her. "Okay. Car wash. Marching band. Homework. Football. Turnaround Formal."

"No," she sighed. Then she stopped for a minute. "Wait. I mean, yes." In spite of all the crazy thoughts crisscrossing through Kat's head, a terrific idea for a routine was coming through. She sat up and brushed her bangs away from her eyes. "That's what our next show should be about. Girls having to ask guys to this dance."

Gabe jumped up and started to pace. He grabbed a pencil off her desk. "We could have a guy sitting by his phone, praying for some girl to call."

"I could be Patty Prom Queen," Kat nodded, making notes, too. "She could be really sure that the guy she's going to ask will say yes, and then he shuts her down."

Gabe laughed. "We could have the lounge lizard give advice to the prim society lady on how to ask a guy out!"

"YES!" Kat said, jumping up and slapping palms with Gabe. Then they were both quiet for a moment, crouched over her desk and jotting down their ideas.

After they'd scribbled for a few minutes, Gabe looked up and Kat met his eyes. He smiled. She looked back down at her notes, then tapped her pen against the desktop. "So what advice would you give?" she added in a much softer voice.

Gabe put his pad away and assumed his lounge lizard posture, a little hunched over, with his eyes half closed and his mouth open.

"No." Kat slapped his arm. "Not some character, Gabe. You."

"Me?"

"You know about stuff like this." She took a deep breath. "What advice would you give on how to ask a guy out?"

His green eyes widened. "You want my advice? My real advice?"

Who else's advice am I going to get? Kat wanted to plead. Miranda had never had to approach a guy, because even before Eric, great guys had always waited in line to ask her out. Jojo's style was a little brash, even for Kat. At least Gabe shared Kat's sense of humor, and he understood the guy's way of seeing things.

Gabe shook his head and looked out the window. "I don't know. I gave advice to Chip yesterday, and it didn't seem to do him much good."

"Chip?"

"Chip wanted Lisa Avery to ask him to the dance."

"Oh, yuck."

"Oh, yes. I probably should have just told him to forget it, but I figured, why not give it a try?"

Why not give it a try? Kat repeated to herself. It's about time.

Gabe shrugged and turned around to face her. "Okay. If you're really serious, then let's give this a shot." He stuck his hands into his pockets, then took a deep breath and rocked on his high-tops and looked away. "So, who are you going to ask?"

"I don't know if I'm going to ask anybody," Kat fired back. "I just said, *if* I were going to ask somebody, what would I say?"

"Don't get touchy."

"Sorry."

"All right." He thought for a moment, then faced her and put his hands on her shoulders. "The important thing is that you can't just come right out with it. That's the mistake Chip made. The mood has to be right."

Kat rolled her eyes. "How can I count on the mood being right when I'm probably going to run into the person right after swimming when I'm all wet and I'll look like someone shrunk my head?"

"You can make the mood right anytime, even if you have a shrunken head." Gabe snapped his fingers. "Okay, say it's after school, and you're waiting on the front lawn for your mom to pick you up to go to the dentist. Is that unromantic enough?"

"Probably."

"Ready?"

"Ready."

"Let's run with it."

They flopped down next to one another on the floor, their legs stretched out. Gabe began watching an imaginary street, and pretty soon he was making the noises of bypassing cars. Then he started adding sound effects for trucks, motorcycles, and bikes with bells.

When Gabe launched into a police siren, Kat yelled, "Okay, Gabe. Enough. I get the picture!"

"Sorry." Gabe drew his legs up and hugged his knees. He whistled, looking around the room as if he were waiting for a bus. Finally he turned back and stared at her. "Kat," he urged.

"What?"

"I'm waiting for you to make the first move. The girl is supposed to ask the guy, remember? How long am I supposed to wait?"

"Oh, oh right." Kat sat there for a while longer as her curtains fluttered and a dog barked outside. She finally allowed herself to think about Brent Tucker's golden hair, his forgiving blue eyes, and the way he'd gently touched her shoulder. Half of her was terrified to feel this way again, while the other half of her was starting to get woozy.

"So, do you know this guy very well?" Gabe suddenly asked.

"What guy?"

"This guy you're going to ask to the dance. What's he like?"

"He's just a guy! And I don't know if I am going to ask him, or anybody! I just wanted some advice."

"Okay, okay. I just wanted to know who I

was supposed to act like. So I'm just a guy. I can do that. I can be just a guy."

"Thanks."

After another pause, Gabe nudged her. "Kat. Come on."

"Right," she mumbled. "Here I go." She cleared her throat and put her head down. She pushed back memories of Grady and thought about Brent instead. "So, um, I bet you've already got a date for the Turnaround Formal, right?"

"No. Wrong." Gabe interrupted, turning to face her. "Dinosaur breath. Start over."

"Why?"

Gabe crossed his arms. "You're as bad as Chip. You have to ease into it. Loosen up. Flirt."

"I hate flirting. I refuse to act dumb!"

"Kat, you don't have to act dumb. I hate to tell you, but what's really sexy is when girls act smart."

"Oh."

He pulled her to her feet. "Okay, just do something crazy, something that has nothing to do with asking me for a date and worrying about whether or not I'm going to say yes." He thought for a moment. "Ask me to dance."

She almost laughed. "Who wants to dance on

the school front lawn while they're waiting for their mother to take them to the dentist?"

"Just ask me to dance," Gabe whispered.

She controlled the urge to scream.

"Kat."

"Okay, okay. Wanna dance?"

"Sure."

Gabe started to move around first, and then Kat bounced a little, too. They clowned, dancing as if they were spaced out stoners at a rock concert. Then they made fun of some of the sillier new dances going around. The breeze blew, and the ocean air swirled around the room. Finally Gabe held out his arms and Kat joined him for a formal foxtrot. Then they moved more slowly, taking easy, boxlike steps. Kat laughed. But they kept on dancing, and their moves started to become more fluid and real.

Gabe dipped Kat in a corny tango, and then she led him into a twirl under her arm. Coming out of the twirl they got all twisted up for a moment, but this time neither of them laughed. Their eyes met, and their arms dropped to their sides. They stared. Neither of them even smiled. Kat suddenly felt like she was a broken record that has stopped on the very best part of her favorite song. Everything normal had been sus-

pended. She could have been standing on the
ceiling or shooting down the old roller coaster
by the beach.

Gabe closed his eyes and took a step in again.
His arm slipped around her back. His other hand
slipped behind her waist, and then both of her
hands were around his neck, and they weren't
moving at all. They were just breathing and
holding each other with incredible sweetness and
care. Every inch of Kat's skin was taking in sensation. Soft, curly hair. Warm, smooth skin.
Well-worn T-shirt.

Suddenly Kat became aware that she and
Gabe — GABE! — were standing in her bedroom wrapped in each other's arms, not moving
or joking or talking or anything. She couldn't
swallow. She could barely breathe. She finally
managed to whisper, "What now?"

"What?" he mumbled in a fuzzy voice.

"Do I ask now?"

"You mean you want to ask me?"

"Do I what?"

"The dance. You want me to go to the dance
with you?"

"What, Gabe? What about the dance?"

"Oh. No. Of course you don't."

"What?"

"Nothing. Never mind."

Now it was like they were speaking different languages. They looked down, and let each other go.

Kat turned away, making a move to open her window until she saw that it was already open. She felt dizzy, confused, and shy, as if Gabe had been transformed into a stranger.

Gabe shoved his hands into his pockets and moved toward the door. "I guess we'll . . . uh . . . finish work on our routine at lunch tomorrow. I've got to go."

"You do?"

He nodded. "I . . . have to go . . . down to the beach and play some volleyball. I told Amy Zandarski I'd come and play." He fidgeted. "You know Amy asked me to the Turnaround dance."

"She did?"

"Shelley Lara asked me, too, but I'm not going with either of them. I don't want to tie myself down. You know me."

Kat's senses were starting to calm down. She saw Gabe again, her dear friend, Gabe the flirt, holding onto her door as if he were going to rip it off and take it with him. "I know you, Gabe. Of course I know you. You're one of my best friends."

"That's right," Gabe said, pointing at her. "We're just friends. You're almost my best friend. You remember that."

"I know. You remember it, too."

"I will."

"Okay."

"Okay!"

They stared at each other for one more totally bizarre moment until Gabe left and Kat crumpled onto her mattress and hugged her pillow to her chest.

ELEVEN

"Eric Geraci goes into his windup. He's check-ing the bases. He's spitting on the ball. Ugh, it's not a pretty sight."

"Gabe, could you stop talking for two sec-onds? I can't concentrate."

"Jojo Hernandez is at the plate, and she can't concentrate. She has a lot of nerve complaining about my commentary when she is not exactly known for keeping her mouth shut. Uh-oh. She's going to take a swing. She's reaching for it. My God! She hit it! It's going, it's going, it's gone!"

"Hey, Miranda," said Kat, who was sitting at their regular lunch table the next Friday, watch-ing their friends goof their way through a make-shift baseball game on the grungy quad.

Miranda didn't look up from her chemistry book.

Jojo hit a home run."

s nice," Miranda murmured.

Eric, Gabe, Jojo, and Chip, along with some of Eric's senior friends, had practically taken over the overcrowded quad. Eric had been pitching a balled-up piece of tinfoil, which Jojo had just batted onto the cafeteria roof with her French book. Chip was playing catcher, and Gabe had been offering a running commentary while playing the infield.

"How come you and Gabe aren't doing your show today?" Miranda asked.

Kat chewed on her yogurt spoon. "Gabe has the whole studio set up to record a music tape for the car wash. So we decided to skip the show this week. We're doing a routine about the Turnaround Formal. It'll be better to do it next week, right before the dance happens." She shifted and bit her lip. "We don't have to do a show every single week, you know."

"I know. I just miss it. I love your show."

"Thanks. It's no big deal."

"Okay." Miranda didn't know why Kat was sounding so defensive. She'd almost had the sense that Kat and Gabe had been avoiding one another all week. "Is everything okay with you and Gabe?"

"Sure. Of course."

Miranda stared at Kat, then decided to leave it at that. Between the car wash, her chem test that day, and Eric's game that night, there were way too many other things on her mind.

"Miranda, come play with us!" Eric called after Jojo leaped over bodies and books to complete her run around the quad. He was crunching another piece of foil into a baseball.

"I can't." Miranda stared at her book. She was beginning to feel that if she took her eyes off the chemical compounds, the rest of her crazy thoughts would explode all over the quad. The unsteady feeling was back in full force, and she wasn't sure why. "I have my chem test fifth period."

Jojo flew into a stag leap and landed on the notebook that stood for home plate. The red-and-white skirt of her cheerleading outfit flared as she fell against David Ronkowski, one of Eric's senior buddies who was in debate.

"YAYYYYYY!" Jojo cheered.

The next batter stepped up, but Eric didn't go into his windup. Instead, he watched Miranda with his hands on his hips. "Hey, David, can you take over for me?" he said when she wouldn't look up at him.

David tore himself away from Jojo, caught the tinfoil ball, and took over as pitcher.

Miranda glanced up as Eric walked over. He looked purposeful and handsome in his jean jacket, Levis, white shirt, and cowboy boots. When he sat down next to her, she could smell licoricey aftershave. She stared back down at her book. Kat quietly got up and moved to the retaining wall.

"Miranda, come on and play," Eric urged. "I have a big game tonight, and I can take it easy and have fun. At least you can try to look like you can have a good time, too."

"Eric, I'm studying. You sound like my father."

"You've been studying all week. You worried about this test all last weekend. You'll do fine."

Part of Miranda knew that Eric was right. But she just wanted to cram more into her head. She didn't want to leave room for stray thoughts about anything else.

Eric whispered, "Listen, Jojo told me she talked to someone on the dance committee. We're up for Princess and her Shining Knight at the Turnaround dance. Isn't that great?"

"We are?" Miranda had forgotten about Princess and her Knight, which were the prom king and queen of the Turnaround Formal. Winning was a huge honor. Princess and her Knight were announced at the dance and awarded to the most high-powered, attractive couple in school. "You think the dance committee might pick us?"

"I'm sure it depends on if I can win again tonight and what other couples show up. I'm amazed at how many people haven't made their dates yet." Eric looked back at the baseball game. "But I think we have a very good shot."

Miranda shrugged.

Eric leaned closer. "Unless nobody sees us together, and they all forget we're a couple."

"I don't think there's any chance of that," Miranda bristled. "Not after they see today's issue of *Bay News*."

"What?"

"This just came out this morning." Miranda pulled that week's newspaper out of her notebook. Sarah's photo of her and Eric kissing on the football field was smack in the middle of page two. At least Jackson had managed to keep them off the front page.

"This is great!" Eric cried, grabbing the paper and looking it over with a huge grin. "It's perfect. Don't you think so?"

Miranda didn't know why nothing seemed

perfect to her anymore. Eric, the baseball madness, their lovey-dovey picture in the paper —
it wasn't just making her feel unsteady, it was
starting to drive her nuts. But the only thing she
could pinpoint was that photo. Couple of the
Year.

Eric was still beaming over their picture. "It's
great timing for Princess and her Shining
Knight."

"I guess." Miranda had felt this same way
when she'd visited Stanford. Her dad had gone
on and on about studying law. Pretty soon he
was talking about how Miranda was going to
be a hot-shot lawyer, too, and how she and Eric
would open a practice together. For the first
time, making a plan had stopped up Miranda's
brain, as if she'd been set in concrete. She'd begun to think, Wait a minute, when did I say I
wanted to be a lawyer? What if I suddenly decide
I want to make tofu with Chip or go into comedy with Kat? And when did I tell you I wanted
to stay with Eric forever? Just who are we talking
about here?

And then all week, she'd walk past the newspaper office and feel like the school roof was
going to fall on her head. At least she hadn't seen
Jackson since their argument, and if she was

lucky, she wouldn't see him until her next junior class report was due.

Eric put the newspaper down and looked at her instead. When she didn't return his open gaze, his brown eyes and strong, clean-shaven face clouded. But before either of them said anything else, the bell rang, ending the lunch period.

Miranda stuffed her books into her briefcase. "I'm sorry. I'm just worried about this test. I'll be fine as soon as fifth period is over."

He stood up, too. "I understand. At least I think I do." He caught her arm and pulled her to him, then stopped when his face was only inches from hers.

Miranda connected with the need in his eyes, but she just wanted to run to class. She gave him a quick press of the lips with her eyes open and her mind on other things. He held onto her after she'd pulled back.

"HALL KISS," they said at the same time, turning it into a joke. Hall kiss was Eric's name for a kiss where they held back, in case a teacher was looking.

"I'd better go." Miranda gestured to Kat and Jojo, who were waiting for her at Jojo's locker.

Eric nodded. But he didn't let go of her hand

until their arms were fully outstretched. "Good luck on your test."

"Thanks."

"See you at the game tonight."

Miranda pulled her hand out of Eric's grasp and quickly joined her two girlfriends. Kat was leaning against the locker next to Jojo's, while Jojo held up a mirror and redid her lipstick.

Miranda hugged her briefcase and tried to get her thoughts back in order. Chem test. English comp. Car wash meeting. Eric's game. "I'll see you both right after school today for the quad project meeting," she reminded Kat and Jojo. "Don't forget. We only have a few more days before the fund-raiser."

"We'll be there," Kat promised. "Never fear."

"Good." Miranda started toward the science rooms. "See you right after school then."

"Hey, Miranda, where are you going?" Jojo suddenly yelled.

Miranda stopped in the middle of the hall. She was jostled and almost swept off by the noisy crowd. "Where do I always go after lunch? I have a test."

"But it's Friday." Jojo acted like the word *Friday* was supposed to set off some kind of alarm.

"I know it's Friday," Miranda hollered back. "That means tomorrow is the car wash, the dance is in a week, and I have four and a half minutes before my chem exam."

"DON'T YOU REMEMBER? YOU HAVE THAT FRIENDS IN NEED ORIENTATION FIFTH AND SIXTH PERIODS TODAY!" Jojo screamed.

Miranda froze in the middle of the crowded hall. She hadn't thought about the Friends in Need orientation since she'd checked the activity board the day they'd snapped her and Eric's picture for the paper. She stood there motionless while lockers slammed, books dropped, and people rushed around her. She'd forgotten her things-to-do list that week. How could it have slipped her mind?

"Miranda," Kat called out. "Are you okay?"

Miranda managed to nod.

"Look on the bright side," Jojo cheered. "Now you won't have to take your chemistry exam!"

Miranda was late getting to the band room. She rushed in with her briefcase open and her blazer stuffed under her arm. But even though her mind was still on a dozen different things, she knew the minute she walked in that she was out of her element. All her studying, her friends, her grades, her father, and Eric wouldn't mean a thing to some of the people who were gathered for the orientation workshop for Friends in Need.

"Everybody grab a chair and form a circle," announced Mr. Newcomb, the young guidance counselor who wore a leather vest and jeans and was liked by most of the student body. He was moving the last of the music stands aside. The piano and the other instruments had been pushed against one wall. "We don't have much time. Let's hurry and get started."

Miranda grabbed the first chair she saw and shoved it into the circle, between a gawky freshman and Eric's and Jojo's friend, debater David Ronkowski, the only person she knew at all well. David smiled at her. Miranda was still so stunned to realize that she was in the band room and not the chemistry lab, that she couldn't quite get her bearings.

Right away Mr. Newcomb got into the middle of the chair circle. "Welcome all. I'd just like you to put your books away and relax. Our student counselors from last year are having their own meeting next door, but they'll join us soon.''

Miranda was still disoriented. It had been so long since her homeroom teacher had selected her for this. Her teacher had said that Mr. Newcomb wanted kids from every walk of Crescent Bay High life. They'd certainly succeeded in that, Miranda realized, as she took in the four representatives from each class. One boy had a pink streak in his hair, and one girl wore black leggings so overly ripped that there was more hole than tights. But then there was Jeff Yakimora from the soccer team, student body president Roslyn Griff, a GQ type named Arnie Wheeldon, and debate champion David.

"This afternoon is about getting to know each other. Being at ease with new people is part of what being a Friends in Need counselor is about," Mr. Newcomb continued. "We need students who are warm and trustworthy, who care about others, and are interested in their personal growth. A Friends in Need counselor should be supportive. You should be trustworthy. And you should have the judgment to recognize problems that you can't handle and refer them to professional therapists."

Miranda finally closed her briefcase and stuck it under her chair. Roslyn looked fascinated. The girl with the torn tights scratched her nose.

"What a Friends in Need counselor should *not* be is judgmental or preachy," Mr. Newcomb went on. "A Friends in Need counselor does not try to change people or put people down." He held up his hands. "But we'll talk more about all that when we actually get into the training later in the semester — if you all decide to stick with this."

Miranda glanced at the clock.

Mr. Newcomb gestured for them all to stand up. "Why don't you all stretch out while we get ready here. Today is just your first orientation, and mostly I want to introduce the idea of getting to know people in a real way and developing trust. We'll do some group exercises that should be fun and may even seem silly, and then we'll be joined by our experienced peer counselors for a more in-depth trust exploration."

They began by introducing themselves in ten words or less. That was easy. Miranda Jamison. Junior class president. After that, the sillier stuff began. They had to repeat every person's name in the circle. They each had to tell a joke. Then they had to form groups of four and let their bodies go limp, trusting that the other three people would catch them before they hit the floor and cracked their heads. Lastly, Mr. Newcomb announced something he called a Scavenger Hunt. He passed out sheets of paper with twenty statements like *Someone who has the same colored eyes as you. Someone who loves to laugh.* The assignment was to match a person to each statement and have the person sign on that line.

Miranda took her Scavenger Hunt sheet and began shuffling around the room.

Someone who has the same color eyes as you — a freshman named Richard Howard signed.

Someone who watches less than five hours of TV a week — Rosyln Griff.

Someone who is not afraid to cry — Naomi Frey (the girl in the torn tights).

Finally Miranda found David Ronkowski and put her paper in front of him. David was signing number five — *Someone who likes to sing in the shower,* when Mr. Newcomb opened the band room door to let in about ten more people.

"Keep working on your Scavenger Hunt," Mr. Newcomb instructed. "The experienced counselors are joining us, and I'd like them to each choose a new person as their partner for the second half of our orientation. We have more new counselors than old, so a few of you new folks may have to pair up with each other."

Good, Miranda thought, sticking close to David.

"Reach out for the person closest to you," Mr. Newcomb commanded. "That's your partner."

Miranda thrust out her hand to tap David. But just as David smiled and reached back for her, someone grabbed her fiercely from behind.

Miranda spun around.

It was Jackson Magruder.

TWELVE

"Close your eyes."

"Why do I have to close my eyes?"

"That's the way this exercise works, Miranda. Okay, don't close your eyes. But you have to put on this blindfold, so it won't matter if your eyes are closed or not."

"Then what?"

"You heard Mr. Newcomb. I'm going to lead you on a blindfolded walk around the campus. I'm not going to kidnap you and throw you in a car trunk."

"Sure."

"Look, do you want to do this, or would you rather just go back to class?"

"This is so pointless. What could possibly be the point of this?"

"Does everything have to have a point?"

"Fine. If this is what Mr. Newcomb wants us

to do, I'll do it. Just give me the blindfold, and let's get it over with."

Jackson reached up to tie the band of white cloth across Miranda's face, but she wrenched it out of his hands. They eyed each other suspiciously, standing on the edge of the quad while other Friends in Need pairs were already smelling the flowers and listening to the wind.

Finally Miranda wrapped the blindfold around her head and tied it. Her glossy hair got bunched up in back, and the blindfold was on crooked. Jackson had to step back for a moment and smile. For the first time since he'd started Crescent Bay High, Miranda didn't look quite so perfect.

"Can you see?"

"Of course I can't see. I'm blindfolded."

"All right." Jackson reached for her hand, but she pulled it away from him. She felt her own way with outstretched arms. She headed right for a pole.

"Watch it," he warned, intercepting her before she crashed.

She jerked away from him and kept going. But when she almost stumbled over a milk carton, her fists clenched, and she let out a little cry.

"Hold onto me," he ordered.

"I can do this by myself."

"You can't do this by yourself, Miranda. You can't see. That's the whole point of this exercise, to let someone else be your eyes. To trust and find a new way of seeing things. Remember?"

Finally she pinched his sweatshirt sleeve as if it were something dirty, carefully avoiding contact with his bare skin. He led her toward the gym.

"Where are we going?" she demanded.

"You'll find out when we get there. Just relax."

Jackson knew he was pushing hard, but as soon as he'd spotted her in the orchestra room, he'd been unable to resist shaking things up again. He still felt that Miranda was the last person who should have been recommended for Friends in Need, and something about her still made him crazy. He told himself that it was because of Leanne. After that conversation with Leanne, he'd realized that peer counseling couldn't just be another accomplishment on Miranda's college applications. It was too important to be crammed between club meetings and extra-credit reports.

"You know, you don't have to do this," he said as they neared the open door of the gym and heard the squeaks and pops of a fast basketball game.

"Of course I have to do this."

"This isn't some required assignment." He could feel her resentment through the fabric of his sweatshirt.

"I said I'd do this, and I'm doing it. I don't give up on things. If I start something I always finish it. Okay?"

"Okay." He still wondered about Leanne and if he should have said something to Mr. Newcomb about Leanne's living on her own. But he knew that Leanne hadn't wanted him to tell anyone, and she didn't seem on the verge of some kind of breakdown or suicide. She'd also left him another note saying that she'd found a job washing dishes at the Tucker Resort and wouldn't need to talk to him again.

"You know, Miranda," Jackson told her, "someone might come to you with a serious problem."

"And walking around with a piece of ripped bed sheet over my eyes is really going to help."

Jackson took a deep breath. He held her shoulders and made her face the gym door. "Hear the B ball game? Just listen."

"Of course I hear the basketball game."

Mr. Newcomb had said that listening was the most important thing about being a peer counselor. He'd told them to give up their eyes for this hour and rely on their ears and their other senses. But Miranda didn't seem to be relying on anything, except her desire to prove that Jackson couldn't get to her. Jackson stood there for a few minutes, while Miranda folded her arms and huffed.

"Come on," he said, leading her away from the gym and deciding to try something much more provocative. If he was going to let her know how to relate to a person like Leanne, he was going to have to shake things up a little more.

He led her behind the cafeteria, where the old lunch smells hung in the air. They went around the auditorium, through the student parking lot, and onto Holiday Street. It wasn't until they reached the stoplight at the corner of campus that her arms stiffened again and she pulled away. He swept one arm around her back and grabbed her wrist, to make sure that she didn't step into the busy street.

She tried to wrestle away from him, reacting to the sound of the cars whizzing by. "Where are we? We're not supposed to leave campus!"

"We're not going far."

"What are you doing?" She reached for her blindfold, but before she could untie it the light turned green.

Jackson knew that he was taking a risk, but something inside him didn't want to turn back. He thought of Leanne again as he slipped his hand around Miranda's and pulled her into the crosswalk. Her slim, graceful body jolted until she finally started to run with him until they were on the other side.

Jackson quickly guided her away from campus while the cars and trucks rumbled past. They walked by the mini-mall where kids bought junk food, past a dentist's office, and a parking lot. Behind that was a sandy vacant lot, and that was where Jackson was headed.

"Why are you doing this?" she demanded with a little less force.

Jackson wondered if she were starting to break down a little. "Why do you have to have a reason for everything?"

"Because I'm a reasonable person. I'm trying to do this assignment. I don't like not being able to see. Can't we just get this over with?"

Her hands went up to the blindfold again, but she didn't rip it off. Jackson was beginning to sense that even though she hated him and the walk, she wouldn't let herself quit. Part of him had to admire her intensity and her will.

He led her across little hills of sand, clumps of reeds, and a few muddy holes. Jackson had discovered the lot on one of his skateboard rides downtown. There was nothing special about it, but he liked the lumpy dunes, and there was one mound that gave a perfect view of the ocean.

"Where are we now?" she asked, her voice betraying a hint of vulnerability.

He had to slip his arm further around Miranda to guide her around the rocks. She was beginning to hold onto him with a little less resistance.

Jackson took her up on the tallest dune and stood behind her, taking his hands off her as the wind blew her long hair against his face. "Can you smell the ocean?"

She didn't answer.

"Can you feel how the air here is special. I'm not sure why, but it is."

She stood there like a blindfolded ghost.

"Miranda, I'm just trying to help," Jackson said.

When she still wouldn't answer, he turned her around, and saw the wet spots on her blindfold and the tears leaking down her face. She was weeping! He looked at her trembling mouth and messy hair and he wanted to press himself against her and hold her as hard as he could.

But she pushed away from him, catching her foot on a clump of reeds, stumbling until she fell hard against the cold sand. She let out a sob and finally ripped off her blindfold.

"I'm sorry," he gasped, dropping to his knees and staring at the tears streaming down her face. "I didn't mean — "

She batted him away. "Yes, you did! You meant everything."

As he watched her tremble and sob, he couldn't believe it. Miranda Jamison would never cry, expecially in front of him. "You're always so sure of everything, and I just wanted to show you that you can't always be that way."

"What makes you think I'm sure of everything?" she screamed, clambering to her knees and not bothering to wipe off the sand. "*You're* the one who's so sure of everything. You're the one who pegs people and thinks you know just who other people are!"

"I — "

"Is this how you help?" she ranted. "Is this how you're so sensitive and warm?"

He felt guilty and stupid.

"Is this how you don't make judgments or try to change people?"

"I just wanted to get through to you."

"What makes you think that you are the person to get through to me? You sit there so smug and self-important, and you have no idea what goes on inside my mind."

"So tell me," he urged, grabbing her arms again before he even knew he'd done it. "Tell me!"

She smacked into him with her shoulder, as if she wanted to knock him down, too. Then she let out another cry and for one moment their eyes locked, and he saw her deep intelligence mixed with a terrible confusion and feelings so strong that neither of them knew quite what was going to come out.

She stood and stumbled back, then scooped up the discarded blindfold and threw it at him. "I'm going back to the band room." She began tearing across the vacant lot, then turned back and pointed at him. "I don't want your help. I don't want anyone's help. I don't want any other person telling me who I am!"

Miranda began running, and all Jackson could do was follow.

THIRTEEN

It was a perfect day for a car wash. Clear, blue sky. Hot sun. Gabe's car-wash tape blared, every song lyric having to do with cars or washing. They'd been there since dawn, taking over the Crescent Bay High parking lot as if they were setting up the fund-raiser of the century. By ten, sponges were being tossed. Dustbusters thrummed. Hoses were uncoiled, and music blasted nonstop as juniors raced across the black-top carting buckets, bottles, and rags.

"Jojo, I can't hear you over Gabe's music tape."

"It's not that, Kat." Jojo cleared her throat. "I think I lost my voice last night."

"It's not possible," Gabe joked, switching into his cool deejay tone. "Jojo without a voice is like me without a voice. And if I lost my voice, the female student body would quit school in protest."

Kat rolled her eyes. "I can believe you're hoarse, Jojo, after last night's game."

"Actually, my voice was okay for the game." Jojo giggled. "It was all that screaming afterwards at the Wave that really got to me."

Gabe nodded and moved to the music.

The three of them were whipping around the inside of their first car of the day, the math teacher's station wagon. While Gabe's car-wash music medley blasted over a pair of speakers set on top of Chip's parked van, they wiped and spritzed, dusted and vacuumed. They spit-shined and made sure to get every nook and cranny.

"I still can't believe we won again last night and that next week we go all the way to Harborville to play for district," Jojo said as she finished cleaning the rearview mirror and climbed into the backseat to do the windows. "Marilyn Canter said that she heard that the Harborville team is really nervous about us." Her voice cracked, and she put a hand to her throat.

"I'm nervous about this Dustbuster," Gabe said from the back cargo area. He whacked the vacuum with his hand. "I'm not sure if it's cleaning up dirt or spitting it back out." He turned

the Dustbuster on Jojo's sweater, making it hike
up to reveal her bare back.

Jojo giggled.

Kat stopped wiping the dashboard. "Gabe, do
you always have to be Mr. Macho Jerk? We have
some serious work to do here."

"Who do you think you are? Miranda?" Gabe
shut off the vacuum and looked at Kat. "Well,
excuuuse me for living. I was just fooling
around." He looked back at Jojo. "Was I being
a jerk?"

"Gabe."

"Kat, I'm asking Jojo's opinion. You called
me a jerk. I value your opinion. Jojo, was I just
being a jerk?"

Jojo looked back and forth between Kat and
Gabe. Personally, she had just finished a delight-
ful week in which she'd gotten a B plus on a
French test, cheered a winning football game,
asked David Ronkowski to the Turnaround
dance and — with the exception of English
class — hadn't once run into Leanne Heard or
any other person who made her feel like a
squashed speck on someone's windshield. She
wasn't going to ruin her lucky streak by getting
into the middle of whatever was going on with
Kat and Gabe. "If you ask me, you've both been

acting weird all week. Now let's get to work. We have four hundred dollars to raise here. The seniors raised four hundred and ten."

"We have not been weird," Kat said, going back to scrubbing the dashboard. "Have we?"

Gabe shrugged. "We're always weird." He went back to his vacuuming.

"Well, something is sure weird with Miranda, too," Jojo said, forcing some volume into her croaky voice. "I'm worried about her. If my boyfriend were captain of a team that had just tied for district, I wouldn't suddenly be moping around like I was flunking out of school."

When no one responded Jojo scrambled down into the back and picked up crumbs from under the seat. "So what was with Miranda last night?" she asked Kat. "I think Eric was mad that he'd just had this incredible win, and she went right home. I tried to call her this morning, but she'd already left to come here."

Kat paused over the steering wheel. "She just kept saying she had to go home early because of this today. You know how nuts she gets over things like this. Still, I know what you mean. I'm kind of worried, too. Maybe she and Eric had a fight."

"Never." Jojo got up on her knees again and

looked around the station wagon. "Are we done?"

"*Voilà*," said Kat. "Our first contribution to a better quad. May the rest of the student body appreciate our sacrifice."

Gabe gunned his Dustbuster and smiled.

The three of them jumped out.

"The inside's all done, Ms. Cranney." Jojo grinned, escorting the math teacher back behind her steering wheel. "Now drive to where you see Miranda and Chip Kohler holding those hoses. That's where they'll wash the outside. Then you go to the buffing and waxing pit stop way over by the flagpole. Pay on your way out."

"I will. Thank you, Joanne. It looks like you're all doing a terrific job."

"Thank you, Ms. Cranney." Jojo waved the station wagon on to Miranda and Chip, then waited for a clean-cut sophomore to pull up in his parents' big sedan.

"Okay, team," Jojo cheered. "Jump in. Here's our second victim."

They climbed in again and went to work while Gabe's tape medley moved on to a tune about washing the dog.

"So, Kat, are you ever going to ask someone to the Turnaround dance?" Jojo hinted while she sprayed the inside of the windshield. Gabe and Kat were working on opposite sides of the backseat. "Please ask someone. We only have another week."

Gabe glanced back at Kat.

Kat flipped an ashtray into a paper bag.

"Well, I'm pretty happy that I asked David Ronkowski," Jojo chattered. "Now if my friends would just get into gear here, maybe I'd have someone to go shopping with and I wouldn't have to decide on a dress all by myself. I hate doing things alone!"

"Miranda and Eric are going," Gabe said.

Kat slammed the empty ashtray back, then perched her chin on the front seat. "David seems nice."

"He's pretty nice." Jojo tossed back her curls and smiled.

"So how did you ask him?" Kat scratched hard at something that had dried on the upholstery.

"What do you mean?" Jojo checked her face in the rearview mirror. "I just asked him."

"You mean, you just came right out with it? You just walked up to him and blurted out, 'Do you want to go to the Turnaround Formal with me?' "

"Sort of."

Gabe stopped humming.

"You didn't beat around the bush, or do something weird like ask him to dance with you on the front lawn?"

Jojo looked at Kat like she'd lost her mind. "I called him on the phone. I asked to please speak to David, and then I said 'Hi, this is Jojo Hernandez, would you like to go to the Turnaround dance with me?' And he said yes." Jojo wiped a speck of lipstick off her teeth. "Why?"

"Nothing," Kat said, refusing to look back at Gabe and climbing out of the sedan. "Just something I've been thinking about all week."

By that afternoon the car wash was a confirmed hit. So many juniors had turned out to work that some had been sent home. The line of waiting cars stretched all the way to Holiday Street. Miranda and Jojo were the stars of the class, and everyone was having such a good time that even Miranda had loosened up enough to run a sponge relay with Chip, Jojo, and Kat.

"Let's get back to our labor of love," Jojo croaked after they'd won the relay and tossed the sponges back into Chip's bucket. "Come on, Kat."

Kat glanced back at Gabe, who was still

clowning with his Dustbuster, waving it over the next car, Lisa Avery's white VW with a convertible top. "I think I'll stay on my break a little longer," Kat called. "There are plenty of people to help. I'll be back soon."

Jojo smiled, waved to Lisa, and trotted over to help Gabe.

At the same time, Kat scuffed her desert boots against the blacktop and ambled across the parking lot. She always had a weird reaction to girls like Lisa. Part of her envied Lisa. After all, Lisa would never have lost her nerve and her heart just because of one night with an out-of-town boy. And yet, girls like Lisa also made Kat sick, because they *did* have such a casual attitude about guys. How could a girl skip from one guy to another without wondering what the guy felt or collecting a few painful scars?

Even more confusing was the way Kat felt around Gabe since last weekend. Suddenly his dumb flirting really bugged her. She wanted to shake him and say, Stop coming on to every girl you see! I know you don't mean it, and I know you're not really like that. And stop leading those girls on and not thinking about what it means.

Striding on, she decided to leave Gabe to Lisa.

Maybe Gabe would ask Lisa to dance on the quad lawn and see how she reacted. Kat would have loved to have seen that.

Strolling down the line of cars, Kat waved to people she knew, finally arriving at the entrance. Shelley Lara and Kiri Smith were guiding the cars into the parking lot and warning them about the wait.

"How's it going?" Kat asked.

"Great!" cheered Shelley.

"Fabulous," Kiri agreed. "I bet we raise more money than any other class. As usual, Miranda did a great job."

"I'll tell her." Kat looked at the waiting line of cars, and that was when it hit her, as strongly as if a bolt of lightning had just come down and zapped her on the skull. A red BMW had just turned on its blinker and pulled into the end of the car-wash line. Even from four cars away she couldn't miss the license plate. *TUCKER*.

Now Kat wanted to run back to Gabe, hide in Chip's van, or glue herself to Miranda. All week she'd been hoping to run into Brent, praying that she'd be inspired by some clever way to break the ice. She'd even considered drawing a cartoon and sticking it in his locker. She'd run into him three times, but hadn't been able to say more than, Hi, how's it going? How are your classes coming along? With every day she'd waited, she'd known that time was running out.

The BMW pulled into the lot, slowing as Shelley and Kiri crouched to give instructions. Kat put her head down and started to walk back. But as she marched, she saw the line of cars move by her and a flash of shiny red roll up. Brent popped his head out of his car. His golden hair gleamed in the sunlight. He hoisted himself in his seat to lean further and tug the pocket of her shorts. "Hi!"

"Hi." Kat's heart was doing jumping jacks.

"It looks like quite a turnout." He craned his neck to see the front of the line. "I guess I'll have to wait awhile."

"I guess." She was doing it again. All her quick, witty thoughts were hitting a brick wall before they could make it to her mouth. She stood alongside his car, hands in her pockets, rocking on her boots.

"I wish I could have helped with this but I had to work for my dad at the resort this morning. We're getting the ballroom ready for the dance next weekend."

Could that have been a hint?

"But I thought I'd at least come down and get my car washed."

"That's good."

He rolled the car forward as the line finally started to move. "Why don't you get in?" he invited. "I'll give you a lift across the parking lot."

She blushed as he leaned to the other side and opened the passenger door. A moment later they were alone. Just the smell of leather, the hum of a well-tuned engine, and Brent in a blue polo shirt, suspenders, and pleated khaki pants. Even Gabe's music tape was drowned out by the lush classical music coming out of Brent's car stereo.

"What is this?" Kat managed, referring to the music.

Brent sat forward and listened with his eyes closed. He conducted with two fingers. "Chopin. Like it?"

She nodded. It sure was different from Gabe's rock and roll. She continued to listen and couldn't think of anything else to say.

The car crept forward. Kat could see that Lisa's convertible was all the way over at the waxing pit stop. Gabe and Jojo were jumping out of yet another clean car. Kat's heart was still pounding like crazy, but she knew that if she didn't take the plunge now, she never would. Miranda was right. This was her chance to rejoin the world.

"Brent," she blurted out, staring down at her folded hands. "I know I should work my way up to this and make some kind of joke, which I'm usually very good at, but I can't think of a joke right now, so would you like to go to the Turnaround dance with me? It's next Saturday night at the Tuck . . of course — you already know where it is — you decided where it was going to be." Her head swam. "I'm sorry. I'm sure twenty girls have already asked you. And after that interview on the radio I'm probably the last person you want to go to some formal dance with, so just forget I said anything." She reached for the car door.

He leaned over and grabbed her hand.

She froze.

"Yes," he said.

"What?"

"Yes."

"Yes, what?"

"Yes, thank you. I'd like to go. I accept."

"You do?"

"Yes."

After that, Kat sat in his front seat grinning like a fool until they reached the front of the line, where she exploded out of Brent's car and ran smack into Gabe.

"What's going on?" Gabe mumbled, looking back and forth between her and Brent.

"Take very good care of this car," she told Gabe, patting the hood of the BMW. She started to race across the parking lot.

With Gabe gawking and Jojo staring as if a spaceship had just landed, Brent leaned out his window and called, "Thanks for asking me to the dance, Kat. It sounds great!"

Kat ran over to the hose area and pulled Miranda into the privacy of Chip's van. As soon as she slid the van door closed, she threw her arms around Miranda and screamed her head off.

FOURTEEN

Chip was frustrated.

He usually thought of himself as a peaceful person, but since three o'clock he'd been wanting to pick up someone's sparkling clean car and throw it against the gym.

It was all because of Lisa, and what had happened when she'd come by in her little white convertible. Chip had worked with Miranda to swab her car. The whole time he'd kept his gaze on the buckets, the fenders, the glass — everywhere but on Lisa's red hair and sultry face.

But when Lisa's car was almost ready to move on to the buff and wax pit stop, he'd felt two fingers creep up the back of his shoulder. He'd turned around, his damp hair falling over his face, and looked right at her.

"Hi, Charles," Lisa had gloated. "Do you have a date for the Turnaround dance yet?"

Chip had told himself that Lisa was a royal
tease, but she still made his knees go weak. And
he *didn't* have a date.

"No. Nobody's asked me yet," Chip
answered.

"Aw, that's too bad," Lisa had cooed, kissing
a finger and tracing it across his cheek. "I asked
this guy who goes to Contra Costa College. I
was hoping I'd see you there." And then she'd
gone right over to chat with Jojo. Together the
two girls had glanced back at him, pointing and
giggling. Ha, ha, ha.

So even at five o'clock, when the car wash
was almost finished, Chip was still replaying the
scene in his head. Everybody else was wild with
pride over having raised almost five hundred
dollars. They were working on their very last
car, his own van, done for free as a thank-you
for having supplied the music system.

As Chip swept the hose up and down the side
of his van, he glanced back and saw Jojo bound-
ing over, having finished her last car. In her pink
shorts, pink sweater, pink aerobic shoes and
socks, she reminded Chip of a child's stuffed toy.

"Chip! Are you okay?" she was calling. "I've
been wanting to talk to you all day. Can you
believe how much money we made?" She

giggled. "I couldn't believe it when Lisa was such a jerk to you and then came over to tell me about . . . "

Chip couldn't stop himself. He turned away from the van, held the hose like it was a weapon, and pointed it right at her. Up and down he swept, until she looked like she had gone through the wash. Her curls hung in soppy ringlets. Her matching clothes clung to her limbs.

"WAAAAAAAAH," Jojo shrieked.

"WAHOOOOO!" Chip yelled like a crazy man.

But then Jojo picked up the nearest bucket and dumped it over Chip's head. He blinked as the soapy gray water ran down his face and to the ends of his long, blond hair.

"WATER FIGHT, WATER FIGHT!" Kat screamed gaily as she ran over to join the madness, too. She grabbed an empty bucket out of Chip's hand and stuck the hose in to fill it up. Within seconds the water fight had turned into a water war, with battles all over the parking lot. Water, buckets, wet rags, spray bottles were all squirting and slapping, flinging and flying through the air.

"Where's Miranda?" Kat yelled, grabbing another full bucket and looking around. But before she could dump it, someone climbed on top of Chip's van and sprayed her from above.

Miranda didn't answer Kat's cry. But she wasn't far away. She was crouching on the other side of Chip's van, avoiding the water fight, even though she knew she wouldn't be safe for long. She was already half-drenched, but after the walk with Jackson, she'd been holding herself in check. If the sand rolled away under her feet again, she felt like she might fall into the center of the earth. She didn't want to do anything that involved screaming or fighting, crying out or letting go.

But on the other side of the van, the water fight intensified. There must have been twelve people dousing each other, throwing sponges, slinging wet towels, and emptying buckets. Every hose was on, and the screams could probably be heard all the way downtown. Kat's giddy laugh was the loudest of them all. That was a sound that Miranda clung to. Kat sounded as delirious as she had when she'd told Miranda about her date with Brent. Kat's happiness and the car-wash success were the two things that made Miranda feel strong.

Miranda considered slipping into the van again. But she didn't think she'd get away with it — wet sponges were starting to fly over the van roof, along with water and an empty bucket. That was when she heard his voice. For some reason it cut through all the laughter and screams.

"Miranda," he said.

Miranda looked. Jackson was standing a few feet away. She'd seen him at the car wash earlier, over at the wax pit stop, and she hadn't quite believed that he'd shown up to help. She hadn't met his eye, or even acknowledged that he was there.

She stared at him, while more buckets were dumped and water flew around them. Jackson's T-shirt hung below his vest, and his jeans looked like they'd been used to polish mirrors. All night Miranda had thought about what had happened between them. Even while she sat through Eric's winning game, she'd been wondering why she'd burst into tears so easily, why she'd ever agreed to leave the campus with him, why she'd ever allowed things to go so far.

But the most alarming thing now was the look in Jackson's eyes. His arrogance was gone. Miranda was ready for another fight, and she had her argument all planned out. But now she saw sadness and something that almost looked like regret. Before she realized it, she took a small step toward him.

Just then a spray bottle flew over the top of the van and fell down, hitting her wrist before bouncing off and clattering to the ground. It barely stung, but Miranda grabbed her hand out of reflex.

Jackson lunged for her. "Are you all right?"

"Of course I'm all right."

"That bottle hit you."

"I know it hit me. I said I'm fine. I don't know why you're suddenly so concerned."

Then a hose snaked its way around the front of the van until it landed near her feet, the water gushing out. At the same time she and Jackson looked down at it. Part of her wanted to just walk away, but part of her also had the strongest impulse to drench him. Of course, she didn't give in to impulses, so she stared at the running hose and stood perfectly still.

When she didn't make a move, he picked the hose up. She tensed, waiting for him to spray her. "Go on," she goaded.

But he just let the water bubble back onto the ground. Then he stuck his hand in the spray, and for a moment Miranda thought that he was going to take a drink. He didn't. Slowly he lifted the hose over his own head and let the water run down his face.

"What are you doing?" she cried. "You're crazy."

"Maybe I am. But it feels good."

She watched him and got the strangest sensation. It was like watching a little kid who had never seen water before. It was unexpected and unplanned and suddenly Miranda wanted to be that way, too. She wanted to wash all the confusion and doubt out of her head and start over: a new person; no labels attached, no expectations, and no lists. When he finally let the hose go and rubbed his face, she grabbed the hose and held it over her own head.

"What are you doing?" he gasped.

She began to smile as the cold water ran down her hair, her face, her arms. She shivered, then ran the water over her feet, drenching her shoes until they were squishy and cold. Jackson took the hose and sprayed his own shoes, then his legs, then his face again. Finally he turned the hose on her, and sprayed them both, smiling as the water bubbled down her long, drippy hair.

Miranda looked at Jackson, and he looked

back at her as water still ran down their faces. Their eyes stayed glued together, and they both began to laugh.

"Which way do you go home?" Jackson asked her, half an hour later when things had calmed down.

Miranda wondered if it were a trick question, but Jackson's expression was still friendly. The car wash had been cleaned up and the parking lot was just a parking lot again, with the addition of some big puddles and splotches of suds. She was one of the last students there, just like she'd been the first to arrive.

"My house is right on the beach," she admitted. "With all the other fancy, overachiever houses."

He smiled his crooked smile. The big, gray hooded sweatshirt he'd worn for the car wash was still half-soaked. His dark hair was still wet and matted on his forehead. In one arm he carried his old leather bomber jacket, and in the other he cradled his skateboard.

"I can walk home alone." She shivered a little, and her shoes squeaked across the lot. Her hair was knotted and plastered down her back. Her clothes still clung to her and felt like they weighed a hundred pounds. "I'm fine."

"I know you're fine." Jackson stuck with her as they turned onto Holiday Street and passed the mini-mall and the vacant lot. "I just wanted to talk to you. I need to talk to you after yesterday. Would that be okay?"

"I walk down the prom," Miranda finally admitted. "Which way do you go?"

Jackson flipped his jacket over his shoulder. "I live up behind the bluff. But I don't mind going out of my way."

Miranda looked back at the campus. Gabe had gone off with Shelley Lara, and Jojo and Kat had driven home with Chip. Eric had been by earlier to lend a hand, but had gone to a teammate's to watch football videos. "I guess it's okay," she finally said, "Whatever. Let's walk."

They started walking. The late afternoon wind coming off the ocean felt like it could whistle through Miranda's sopping hair. The sun was getting lower, and the air was salty, slightly damp — sailing weather, Miranda's father called it. Miranda felt a little like she was sailing as she strolled alongside Jackson, her shoes leaving little wet blotches on the concrete with each step.

Until they reached downtown, neither of them said another word. But the whole time,

Miranda felt like she was overly aware of Jackson. She watched their strides. His wet tennis shoe. Her sopping loafer. His jeans. Her crisp slacks, now baggy and out of shape. Her breathing seemed loud, her step clumsy; twice she almost bumped into him when they turned a corner.

In almost no time they'd traveled the length of Ocean Avenue and the two of them were standing at the intersection of the prom, where the ocean spread out before them. The wind was definitely stronger here, and Miranda felt the chill.

"Why don't you take my jacket?" Jackson said. He slipped his leather jacket off his shoulder and held it out to her. It was worn in a very comfortable sort of way, with a lamb's wool collar and that soft, earthy smell.

Miranda shook her head. "My house isn't far."

Jackson touched Miranda's arm. "Your lips are turning blue. You'd better take it."

Miranda finally draped the jacket over her shoulders. It was a whole different feel from Eric's letterman's jacket: lighter and softer. They stepped onto the prom. Miranda began to stroll while Jackson rode alongside.

"I wanted to apologize for yesterday," Jackson finally said. "You were right."

"About what?"

Jackson hesitated for a moment, then his words came in a rush. "About me deciding who you were. I did. I decided that you were a certain way the first time I saw you. I'm sorry."

"Maybe I am that way."

"Maybe you're not."

"I couldn't tell you, because I don't know what way I am these days."

"That's okay," Jackson sighed. "Who does know? I think you're better off to admit it, and not have any illusions."

They stopped to let some joggers pass. Jackson scooped his skateboard up under his arm, almost the same way Miranda held her briefcase. He looked at her with a warm smile.

"You know, it's a funny thing," she found herself admitting. She was feeling less cold as she gathered the lapels of his jacket around her neck. "You can think you've got things really figured out and then something surprises you and makes you realize you might want to go a totally different way."

Jackson shrugged. A laugh bubbled out, and he pushed back the sleeves of his sweatshirt. "I guess that's what I was trying to do on that walk, surprise you a little."

"You sure did that."

Jackson nodded, "Yeah, well, you want to know what's really weird?"

"What?"

"You surprised me even more."

His face was so intelligent, curious, but for the first time also open, not arrogant or dismissive. No matter how defensive Miranda still might want to be, she couldn't ignore the warmth in his eyes.

They strolled again, past three-story houses with huge windows and wraparound decks. Within another block they were at Miranda's house, a two-story contemporary with almost a dozen oceanfront windows of different shapes and sizes. Jackson admired the slanted glass and woodwork from the sidewalk. "That's a pretty impressive house," he said. Then he looked up and pointed. "Hey, I like the weather vane on your roof. It's kind of different from the rest of it."

Miranda laughed. "That's an antique my mother put up. It points every which way, and in a storm it really goes crazy. My mom used to be really into antiques. Old painted pigs and tools and quilts."

"Not anymore?" Jackson asked.

"Now she's into having her career," Miranda said, amazed that she was even mentioning this. She didn't even talk this over with Eric. "She had to wait a long time for her career, and my two older sisters are in college. I think it's good that she's doing really well."

Jackson nodded, breaking into his quirky smile. "Another surprise. That's why you have to be ready for whatever happens, because it's all going to happen. Parents change your life without warning you. Everything's always changing."

Miranda looked back at the house and saw her father at the dining room table, talking on the phone. At the same time, he noticed her and came to the kitchen door. Still holding the phone, he opened the door and waved her in.

"I've got to go," Miranda said. She wiggled out of Jackson's jacket and started to shiver again. "Here's your jacket." She cradled the jacket and handed it over. When Jackson took it from her, his hand landed on top of hers and for a moment neither of them moved.

"MIRANDA, WHAT ARE YOU DOING?"
her father yelled.

Miranda pulled her hand away and stepped
back. She looked back at her father, who was
still holding the phone and staring at her. "I have
to go. 'Bye. Thanks for the jacket."

"Any time." Jackson smiled. He set down his
skateboard, then gave it a kick so that it som-
ersaulted, after which he caught it and set it
down again. He started to push off, then recon-
sidered. "By the way, your car wash was great.
I take back all that stuff I said at the assembly.
It'll be really nice to fix up our crummy old
quad."

Miranda laughed.

"Maybe I'll see you around school," Jackson
answered, finally crouching down and riding
back down the prom.

"Maybe." Miranda lingered for a moment,
then turned around and headed up the gravel
path that led to the kitchen door.

Her father was just inside, wearing a sweatsuit, with a pencil behind his ear. His papers were
all over the dining room table, and he was still
on the phone. Miranda tried to tiptoe by.

"Who was that?" he asked, clapping his hand

over the receiver. "And why are you such a mess?"

"I was at the car wash, Dad. Remember?"

Her father looked back out the window. "You were supposed to be washing cars, not each other. Who was that boy?"

Miranda shrugged and went upstairs without bothering to give him an answer.

FIFTEEN

"Brent, we have the final plans for the Ocean Star Ballroom this weekend. I think it's going to look lovely for your high school dance. Would you like to see the drawings? There's only a few days left if you want to make any changes."

"That's okay, George. You take care of it."

"Are you sure? The students who stopped by yesterday seemed eager to know just how everything was going to look."

"I'm sure. Thanks, George. Just leave me alone, okay?"

"Whatever you say, Brent. I'll have the plans in my office. If you change your mind, just come on up."

Spare me, Brent wanted to yell as George Bouchard, the Tucker Resort assistant manager, practically bowed and scurried back across the

Sea Cove Dining Room. It wasn't even five, and Brent was killing time. His older sister and parents had gone up to San Francisco for the whole day. Since it was Wednesday and he'd had school all week, he'd been left behind. After classes that day, he'd gone for a drive, listened to music, and called some of his old friends. Now an iced bowl filled with big, fat shrimps sat in front of him, the best the restaurant had to offer. Brent hadn't touched it.

"Why did I ever have to move here?" Brent grumbled, looking around at the huge wall paintings of sea conches and fan-shaped shells. The style was some weird combination of art deco and Sea World, while the restaurant's enormous big bay window gave a magnificent view of the ocean. But the great view and beautiful surroundings didn't mean a thing. Neither did the tacky tourists or the old amusement park at the other end of the prom.

"Give me city, any day," Brent groaned.

If he were back in San Rafael, he'd have driven into San Francisco and chosen between a hundred movies, two hundred restaurants, a dozen huge record stores, clubs, concerts, and a score of fairly interesting girls. But he wasn't in San Rafael. And besides the ocean, all there was in Crescent Bay was a downtown with maybe thirty stores, a pier with an ordinary teen hangout, and his fellow students at Crescent Bay High.

BORING, Brent printed out on his napkin.

He widened his eyes, looked around the dining room again, and wondered what he was going to do.

He still couldn't believe that Kat McDonough was the *only* girl who'd asked him to the Turnaround Formal. She was nice-looking and funny and all that, but she got soooo jumpy. Brent lost interest when girls were too easy, and he'd hoped for some interest out of this dance. Beautiful Miranda Jamison should have come begging. He'd always been intrigued by those uptight, achiever types. Let their hair down a little and who knew what they would do. At least there could have been some dicey competition for his company, like Miranda and Kat fighting over him. Now *that* might have made things interesting. But he'd probably blown it by coming on like such a simp.

"Just make a good impression," his father had ordered, "Stay out of trouble this time. And don't give me any back talk."

Yes, sir.

Hadn't Brent done everything in his power to make a boring, good impression? Hadn't he bent over backwards to be polite and modest, warm and kind? If he kept it up much longer, he'd be ready for the Boy Scouts.

Brent sighed heavily. He pushed his chair back from the table and stood up. There was no way around it. Staring out at the ocean made him feel like he was dead. He had to move. His whole body felt pent up. He had to get some *edge* back into his life, some danger, some spark.

Without a word to anyone, Brent abandoned his table, walked across the restaurant, and headed back toward the lavish apartment where he and his family lived. And that's when he noticed that the door to the kitchen was propped open. The aroma was enticing, but that wasn't what Brent was interested in. Instead he was attracted by the heat, the movement, and the light. There was also the sharp memory of a girl with white-blonde hair and a striking dark-red mouth.

He stepped in. The stainless-steel counters and cold, hard tiles were in contrast to the smoke and the sizzle. Fish baked in heavy iron skillets, knife blades did a quick *chop, chop, chop* across fresh vegetables, while waiters and cooks were going back and forth, dealing with all the orders.

"Hello, Mr. Tucker," said the chef.

"How are you today, sir?" said his assistant, with a sickening smile.

Brent ignored them and kept looking. He left the smoke and the smell and went back to a room that steamed and churned. And there she was, taking bowls out of a huge dishwasher and stacking them on a shelf. This room smelled like soap and old food. It was hot and humid as the tropics. Brent waved Leanne's fellow dishwasher out of the room, a skinny college kid who fled the minute he recognized Brent's face. Then Brent stood, sweating a little and watching her.

Now Leanne was *interesting*. Brent liked her lush, full body, her pale skin, and bleached blonde hair. It all appealed to him a lot more than those healthy athletic types at school. But mostly he liked that she was sullen and on the outside. No charm would be needed here. No politeness. No games. He could do as he pleased, and whatever happened, it wouldn't get back to his father. And even if it did, she was the kind of girl who would just drive his father crazy, and that suited Brent just fine.

Leanne didn't notice him until she started to leave the dishwashing area. She was loaded down with a stack of salad plates.

Brent blocked her path.

Leanne gasped, then froze for a moment. When he still wouldn't let her pass, she took her plates back to the dishwasher and stuck them above on a metal shelf. Then she went back to work, while he just stared, letting his eyes wander up and down her body. Slim ankles. Full calves. Narrow waist. Round hips. The crazy, absurd thought of showing up with her at the Turnaround Formal brought a smile to his face.

"Hi," he said. His pulse was finally beginning to pick up. "I'm Brent."

"I know who you are," she said, without looking up. "Everyone here knows."

"Good. Because I know who you are, too."

She glanced at him with suspicious eyes.

"Leanne Heard," he recited from memory. "Crescent Bay High junior. Sixteen years old. Five feet four. A hundred and twenty-three pounds. No work experience. No address or phone number. Hm. Mysterious. I love a good mystery."

"How do you know all that?"

He played coy and snapped one of his suspender straps. "I snuck a look at your job application."

She picked up another set of dishes and tried to get past him again. "Let me get by. Please. I don't want to lose my job."

He held his hands out and laughed. "You don't understand. You won't lose your job for talking to me. Around here, you get a promotion for making me happy."

"I'll bet."

"It's true. I'm a very powerful guy. Remember that." He pouted, snatched the dishes from her, and set them on a nearby cart. "I'm also a very lonely guy," he said, blocking her way again. "And a very bored guy. I have the feeling you know what I'm talking about."

She looked down at the floor.

"Oh, come on," he enticed, lifting her chin and making her look at him. He kept his hand on her face. Oh, he liked the angry, sullen look in her wide, gray eyes. "Something about the way you look tells me you're not exactly sweet and innocent. So when are we going to go out? Tonight? Tonight suits me fine. When do you get off?"

Leanne turned away from him but he caught her chin, then slipped his other arm around her fleshy back. His face was only inches from hers. "I'm not working tonight," she managed. "I only came in for a couple of hours." She tried to wrench herself away. "I have to get all these dishes done."

He pulled her in more tightly, enjoying the resistance in her lush body. "I can wait. You make me happy, and you don't have to worry about dishes. You make me mad, and you may not have any dishes to wash at all."

Her eyes opened wide with fear. "What's that supposed to mean?"

"I'll show you what it means." He sharply tugged her face toward his and kissed her hard. She tried to turn her head, so he backed her against the wall, mouth still pressed against her, smiling underneath the kiss. Finally she tried to shove him with her knee, and he had to defend himself and let her go. She stumbled back, her red lipstick smeared, and her eyes filled with rage.

"Leave me alone!" she shouted, backing away.

Brent lunged toward her again and caught her wrist as she tried to twist away from him. Feeling her fine skin twist and turn under his grip was making him feel more alive than he had since he'd arrived in dreary Crescent Bay. Abruptly, when he sensed that she least expected it, he let her go.

Leanne staggered back against the steaming dish machine.

"Don't get all excited," he said in an overly sweet voice. "If you really want to finish your dirty dishes, you just go ahead. I'll just have to go on without you tonight." He dropped his smile and pointed a finger. "But I know where to find you. And don't you worry, Leanne Heard. I'll be back."

He thought he heard Leanne burst into tears as she turned her back on him and went back to her work.

"Shoes. Stockings. Makeup. Strapless bra. Evening purse and some kind of wrap, in case it's cold on Saturday night. What else?"

"What, Jojo?"

"Miranda, you are really starting to turn into a space case," Kat teased. "It's like I have a whole new best friend lately, class president from the planet Pluto."

Miranda laughed.

Jojo, Miranda, and Kat were on the corner of Third Street and Ocean Avenue, in the middle of the downtown shopping district. The air smelled thick and sweet as they stood between Bruce's Candy Kitchen and an indoor mall that contained a small merry-go-round. Organ music thumped faintly as Jojo examined a newly purchased sequined bag, while Miranda stared at the taffy machine and Kat hummed along with the merry-go-round.

"You know, you haven't exactly been your old wisecracker self this week, either," Miranda teased Kat. "I'm starting to wonder if you haven't turned into one of your radio characters."

"It's hormones," Kat tossed back.

"I'm the only consistent person in this trio," Jojo bragged, holding up her shopping bags. "Just let me go shopping and I'm happy."

Miranda went back to staring in the window. Dense, beige taffy stretched and swung on big metal rollers, surrounded by huge tubs and a table covered with a marble slab.

Kat passed her hand in front of Miranda's face. "Hello? Hey, don't phase out on me. Not now, not when I'm finally doing everything you wanted. Not when I feel like tap dancing on the pier and doing stand-up in front of the Aquarium." Kat kissed the top of Miranda's head.

Miranda smiled back at her. "I'm just thinking. And I'm really glad it all worked out with Brent."

"Me, too."

Jojo applauded, then joined them and stuck her chin on Kat's shoulder. "Kat, I told some girls in my English class about you and Brent, and they were drooling with envy."

"Drooling?" Kat teased. She poked Jojo. "All over their English papers?"

"It's what they did." Jojo insisted, giving Kat a nudge. "Now let's get back to the serious business of shopping. The stores will all be closed soon." When neither Kat nor Miranda made a move, Jojo stuck a hand into Miranda's briefcase and pulled out her notebook. She found Miranda's normal things-to-do calendar, but it was completely blank. "Miranda, how come there's no list on here?"

Miranda took back her notebook. "Eric and I bought all our stuff for the dance a month ago, so I didn't need a list. And I guess I've been thinking about other things."

"Really." Jojo grinned. "I'm so nervous about the game tomorrow in Harborville. One more win! One more win! I can't wait. I'm driving over there with the squad. Miranda, is your dad driving, or are you going on the spirit bus?"

"My dad has a big case in Concord. He won't

be back until Saturday. Want to take the bus together?" Miranda asked Kat.

Kat nodded and grinned. Then she tugged Jojo's curls and pointed to Bruce's Candy Kitchen. "What I really want is a giant hunk of the peanut butter fudge. Who wants to join me and stop me from devouring an entire pound?"

"I will," Miranda said suddenly.

"You never eat fudge!" Jojo objected.

"What can I say?" Miranda laughed. "People change."

Jojo backed away, as if they were going to eat arsenic. "You guys pig out without me. I've still got to find a pair of shoes. I'll call you both tonight."

"Jojo, wait!" Kat teased as Jojo hurried up the street. "You've already got more shoes than Princess Diana."

"The ruby slippers," Jojo said to herself. Kat and Miranda were gone, and she'd reached the other end of Ocean Avenue, so she couldn't tell them about her shoes now. She could still think of a hundred different things she wanted to talk about. She still wanted to know more about Brent, and what was *really* going on with Kat and Gabe, and if there was something going off between Miranda and Eric. But since she was on her own, Jojo thought about shoes.

She knew whenever she was really excited about buying a new pair of shoes, because she would flash on *The Wizard of Oz* and Dorothy's ruby slippers. Jojo always knew when she was onto the right pair of shoes because she could hear the Good Witch whispering in her head. "Buy this pair, Jojo. Buy this pair."

Well, she'd heard that voice in the back of her head ever since last Saturday's car wash. The shoes that were making Glinda the Good Witch speak to her were in the window of Anna Laurence's, one of the most expensive boutiques in town.

They weren't ruby, but a pair of green velvet pumps. Jojo was convinced they were shoes she would be remembered by. This was important because Jojo was *not* convinced that her date was going to be great. David was a nice guy, but not exactly *Mr. Hot Number*, like Eric, and certainly not like Brent. When Jojo waltzed into the Tucker Resort on David's arm, it wasn't exactly going to be *People Magazine* pant time. Sarah Donovan wouldn't bother to snap a picture of Jojo and David for the school paper.

That was why Jojo *wasn't* going to compromise on her clothes. Emerald slippers, even though they were expensive and not marked down one cent since Jojo had first walked by a week ago. That was all right. Jojo had a credit card and a healthy monthly allowance from her folks. She knew that Kat and Miranda would be in shock when they saw how much the shoes cost. They wouldn't tell her not to do it, and they wouldn't really even be jealous. They'd simply say to each other "It's just Jojo," the same way they shook their heads about her ability to ferret out great bits of gossip. They were both attracted and repelled by what she could do, kind of like what happened to heavenly bodies in Mr. Podeskar's physics class.

"Actually, I'm kind of attracted and repelled by what I do myself sometimes," Jojo whispered as she walked along.

She was both attracted and repelled by how far she would go just to make popular people like her. She'd been thinking about how mad Chip had gotten during the car wash. Jojo had seen that look in his eyes when he'd aimed the hose at her, as if he'd wished it were a machine gun. At lunchtime now, he wasn't offering to share any of his yogurt with her, usually a ritual

because Jojo was one of the few people in the
group who truly appreciated Chip's taste in
food. Jojo still felt bad about it. She would have
to think of some way to make it up to him.

But not now, because she was standing in
front of Anna's. The tasteful blue-and-gold-
striped awning, the pastel scarves, and the flaw-
less silk dresses in the window told Jojo to prime
her wallet. Within minutes she was in and out
of the store, the only difference being the large
white sack containing the box of shoes and Jojo's
credit card slip.

Since it was still light and her mom was probably picking up one of her brothers at a music
lesson, Jojo decided to walk home. She'd have
to cut through the north end of downtown,
which was definite Kmart territory, dotted by
rundown beach cottages, a few trailer parks, and
crummy apartments. It was definitely not the
part of town the Chamber of Commerce put on
the brochures they gave away to tourists.

Jojo was just getting to the area where downtown blended in with the shabbier residential
area, when she stopped in her tracks. A girl had
just stepped in front of her, wearing an old blue
coat and high heels. She was walking fast, but

it took Jojo barely a second to identify her. *Leanne!*

Jojo hadn't talked to Leanne since that time during the football game. Sure, they saw one another in English class but Leanne would just stare at her while Jojo jabbered, and Jojo would always get the feeling that Leanne was thinking, "You airhead, phony, shopaholic smile queen."

But now Jojo was curious. She followed at Leanne's pace. She didn't follow very long because suddenly Leanne stopped in front of a two-story building. Definitely a place where drunks or other wiped-out people lived, but to Jojo's amazement Leanne was standing there looking like she was digging around for a key in her purse.

Jojo stopped and watched. It wasn't just the potential for gossip that hooked her; it was the bewildering possibility that Leanne could actually live in a place like that.

Finally Leanne found her keys. Sure enough, she went to the door and stuck her key into the lock. Just then a rather loud truck went by and, for some dumb reason, honked at the two girls. Leanne turned around.

Jojo was surprised at the reaction. When

Leanne saw her, she didn't give her usual haughty, defensive look. Instead Leanne just stared. Her makeup was a mess, as if she'd been crying, or wildly making out in the backseat of someone's car.

"Hi," Jojo said, while at the same time not quite believing she was saying it.

Now Leanne reacted. She violently jerked the key out of the lock. "This is just what I need."

"What?" Jojo asked.

Leanne spun around. Her secondhand dress had big splotches that looked like soap or food. "Go away."

Jojo couldn't move. She saw a desperation in Leanne's eyes that wiped thoughts of shoes and dances and football cheers right out of her head.

Leanne walked into the building lobby, which smelled of dirt and urine.

For some reason, Jojo followed her. There she was with two hundred dollars' worth of packages in her arms, plus her brand-new shoes, and she was following a girl who didn't like her. Still Jojo persisted. When Leanne walked past the list of names on the register, Jojo glanced over and saw *2D: Leanne Heard.* No Mrs. Betty Heard; Mr. Walter Heard. Just Leanne.

Leanne glanced back and saw Jojo looking.

"Should I expect a cover story in the school newspaper?" There was more than anger in her voice this time. It was as if Jojo and her big mouth were everything that was wrong with the entire world. "Or maybe you and the cheerleading squad can come up with a new yell for me."

Jojo didn't know what to say. Leanne had gone from pale to red-faced. Tears were starting to form in her gray eyes. Jojo started to back away.

"Just tell everyone!" Leanne finally spat out. "I'm sick of hiding it. I'm sick of all you people in town who have so much money and think you can treat me any way you want." She began to weep. "I've had it with all of you! Just tell everyone this is where I live, and it's because my mother's boyfriend is a slime who hates me and hits me when I won't do what he says. And I hate him, too. Tell your friend Kat to do a show about that on the radio."

Jojo shook her head. "Kat?"

Tears were streaming down Leanne's face now. She grabbed the building's inner door, then turned back. She looked down and rubbed a fresh-looking bruise on her wrist. "Yeah, Kat. And tell her something else, too. Tell her that

Brent guy that you keep gossiping about in English class is an incredible sleaze."

"What?"

"Your good friend Kat is going to that stupid dance with the lowest, slimiest guy in the entire school."

"What do you mean? What are you talking — "

"I DON'T WANT TO TALK TO YOU ANYMORE!" Leanne suddenly shouted.

Jojo froze. For a moment she was unable to move, surrounded by the stale smell, the register, and the smudgy metal mailboxes. But finally she backed away from Leanne and got out of the lobby. Outside, she began running down the street. She ran and ran, clutching her packages until she made it back to the Long's Drug Store and found a pay phone.

But as soon as she lifted the receiver, she put it down again. She wasn't sure who to call. She wasn't sure what to say. All she knew was that for once in her life she wanted to think before she opened her big mouth.

SIXTEEN

Kat held her long black dress up to her strong body. She still couldn't believe she dared to buy it, or that her mother was going to let her wear it. It was a sophisticated black halter dress, slinky and backless, plain except for a touch of satin trim. Kat could see herself accepting an Academy Award in that dress, or sitting down to a candlelight supper in Paris or Rome. It was the kind of dress that could change someone's entire life.

"I can't be cool about this, Miranda," she chattered. "I feel insane. Good insane, but insane. Maybe I should turn this into a new character."

"You look beautiful," Miranda said, "You really do."

Kat glanced back and made a funny face. It was Friday, after school. They were in her second-story bedroom, and Miranda was sitting in

209

the old rocking chair, just under the Lily Tomlin poster. She was surrounded by Kat's mess of books, paper, and her collection of weird stuffed animals.

Unlike Kat, who was nearly bouncing off the walls, Miranda was thoughtful, even subdued. Her hair was in a sloppy ponytail, and she wore soft jeans with a Crescent Bay High sweatshirt under her blazer. Miranda was so still she didn't even rock in the old chair. Sometimes she'd really been there with Kat — admiring the dress, agreeing that Kat was the luckiest girl in the entire world. And sometimes she was somewhere else. She'd been like that ever since they'd met after school and rushed up to Kat's bedroom.

"I'll hurry," Kat promised, turning to look at herself in the mirror again and smoothing down the slinky, slick fabric. She checked her alarm clock that sat on a fruit crate next to her mattress on the floor. "The spirit bus doesn't leave school until four-thirty to go to Harborville for the game. We'll make it back to school in plenty of time. Thanks for coming over here to look at this."

Miranda stared down at her hands. "You really do look beautiful, Kat."

Kat actually *felt* beautiful. "You know what I really like about this dress?"

"What?"

"It's not me."

"What do you mean?"

"It's not a joke," Kat sighed, turning in a circle and watching the hem swirl. "There is nothing funny about this dress. This is a come-and-look-at-me, I'm-a-serious-person dress. And it's an I'm-back-in-circulation dress." She pretended to bite her hand. "Don't you think so?"

Miranda smiled but at the same time Kat could see that she didn't really agree with her. "It's part you, part not you, I guess."

"Oh, no, after all these years, you've finally discovered my split personality."

"Forget the whole thing," Miranda said, going somewhere else again. "I don't know what I mean, I've been thinking about this stuff all week and it still doesn't make any sense."

Kat nodded. "I'm glad to know you've been thinking. I've been wondering where you've been."

Miranda bit her lip. How was she going to explain any of it to Kat? Of all the people in her life, she'd wanted to talk to Kat, but there hadn't been a right time. Either Jojo was around, or her father, or Eric. She'd tried to talk to Eric, too, but he'd just gone on about his big play-off game, wanting to know exactly where she'd be sitting so he could wave to her for good luck. He'd talked about how disappointed he was that her father couldn't come. And when she'd finally tried to change the subject, he just tuned into his second favorite topic — how good a chance they had of winning Princess and her Knight and how great they were going to look together at the dance.

The more Eric had talked, the more Miranda had filled up with questions. Questions about Eric. Question about Jackson. Questions about herself. Questions about the one thing she *didn't* want to question . . . Kat's happiness.

Kat finally slipped off her dress and carefully hung it back in its plastic sack. She marched across the room in her red cotton undies and white bra, then yanked a huge T-shirt out of her closet and pulled it on. "So, Miranda, do you think I should wear my desert boots with this? How about high-tops?" Kat giddily leaned into her closet and pulled out all the shoes she owned — three pairs.

Miranda stared blankly. All week she had been

trying not to think about the dance. She'd avoided Jackson and been fairly normal with Eric, but now the stakes had changed again. She couldn't avoid thinking about the dance anymore because of the previous night's phone call from Jojo. Over and over that phone conversation kept playing in her head.

"Miranda?" Jojo had said in a funny voice.

"Hi, Jojo."

"Hi. Listen, I won't keep you long. I just want to tell you that there might be something weird about Brent."

"What?"

"Don't ask me anything. Just take my word. I heard from someone that Brent might be bad news."

"Who told you?"

"I can't say. I can't tell you any more about it. I would call Kat myself, but I'm not sure if she should know. I don't even know if what I heard is true. But I think it is. You decide whether or not to say something to Kat."

"Jojo, you have to tell me more. . . . "

With that Jojo hung up. And Miranda had gone off to lie in bed and stare at the walls.

Kat was still digging in her closet, flinging out books and clothes as she foraged for her shoes.

"All I have are boring black flats with little teddy bears on them. Maybe I should go barefoot. What do you think?"

Miranda was still playing that phone conversation over in her head. Jojo had been so brief. She hadn't laughed, she hadn't eleborated. It had felt like a *danger* call. What had alarmed Miranda the most was that Jojo wouldn't confess the source.

Miranda rocked harder and stared out Kat's open window as the ocean breeze fluttered in. Jojo never kept a secret. She never shrank from saying who had told her anything. And that's what made Miranda fear that the gossip might be true.

"Or maybe I should wear my junk-collection necklace," Kat rambled. "I could put my nose clip on it and a few pictures of me in the eighth grade when I was chubby and wore braces."

Watching Kat's glee was making Miranda feel sick. Was Miranda going to tell her, Just fooling, sorry I set you up. Forget the whole thing. Brent might just be as big a heartbreaker as that guy you fell for last summer. Sorry I didn't see it sooner, but I've had some heavy things on my mind, too. And besides, maybe Jojo is just blabbing and it isn't even true.

But on the other hand, what if she didn't tell her and Jojo's gossip did turn out to be true?

"How about these?" Kat said, crawling back in her closet and pulling out an ancient pair of ballet shoes. "Do you remember when we took ballet together? I hated those little tutus so much, and remember how Jojo used to show off because she was the only one who could do the splits?"

Miranda looked away. "I always had the steps perfect, but I was the worst dancer in the class."

"You were not."

"I was." Finally Miranda got up from the rocker. She sat down on Kat's mattress and coiled up with her arms around her knees. "Kat, I have to tell you something."

Kat was still going through her closet, sticking her hands into pairs of panty hose and checking them for runs. "Yeah?"

Miranda felt dizzy. This had been her biggest plan of all. If this didn't pan out, where would she stand then? "I know you're really excited about the dance, and I think that's great."

"You'd better think it's great," Kat teased, plopping down beside her with a pile of panty hose, which she continued to go through. "It was your idea."

"I know. But just be careful."

"What?"

"You heard me."

Kat giggled and fell over on her bed. "Miranda, aren't you worrying about me a little too much? Who are you, my mother? Do I have to ask you if I want to kiss Brent on our first date?"

"I just mean, be on your guard."

Kat sat up again. There was a tightness around her mouth and a slightly irritated look in her eyes. "Don't throw myself at him like I did at Grady? Is that what you're trying to say? Be controlled and ultra together like you and perfect Eric?"

Miranda flinched. "I just mean, none of us really know Brent. He's new. Be on your guard."

"Oh, great!" Kat exploded. She threw the panty hose down on the bed and stomped over to the window where she turned back and pointed to Miranda. Her giddiness had been replaced by fury. "Thanks a lot, Miranda. You are just the best friend that every girl should have."

"What do you mean?"

"You push me into this date and then completely flake out when I need you. Now, just when I'm totally high over it, you tell me watch out, we don't know this guy. Be careful. What is your problem?"

"I don't know."

"Well, you'd better find out. Whatever's going on with you, you'd better figure it out before you start losing all your friends."

Miranda hurried back to school alone. After their argument, Kat had suddenly decided to ride with someone from the swim team, as if just being on the same bus with Miranda would make Brent not even show up for their date at all.

Jogging the half mile back to campus, Miranda's brain wouldn't slow down. Any peace and lightness she'd been feeling since the car wash was out the window. She couldn't get her thoughts in order. There were no lists anymore, no new ideas, just crisscrossing, clashing images and ideas that zapped alarm through her and made her crazy. *Jojo's call. Brent. Jackson. Eric.*

"Oh, my God!" Miranda cried, suddenly stopping and looking around. She was on Cliffview Street, in front of a bunch of small vacation houses, down the street from the supermarket and the police station. Clouds were moving in. The air was getting damp.

"I went the wrong way," she realized, turning around in a full circle, then checking the street signs she'd read a thousand times before. She'd gone two blocks out of her way, as if she were going home instead of back to school.

Taking her briefcase off her shoulder and holding it against her chest, she began to run. But she was wearing her stiff riding boots, and she felt anything but quick and springy. When she hit Astor Street she had to stop for the world's longest light. Finally she took off, zigzagging through the cars and almost getting hit.

"Look out!" someone screamed at her.

Someone else honked, and a third person shook his fist.

Miranda didn't care. She kept running until she got back to Holiday Street. Deciding to cut through the middle of campus, she ran in behind the shop classrooms and the new computer room. She tried to cut through the auditorium, but it was locked, so she had to run all the way around to reach the hall outside the library. Past Jojo's locker, across the empty quad. She was getting hot and tired and tore her blazer off one arm as she passed the stairway that led up to the journalism room.

She stopped to catch her breath. Was Jackson

still there? Then she wondered why she was even thinking about Jackson and started running again, past the offices and the trophy case and right into the main doors.

She smacked the doors so hard that her wrist smarted and tears came to her eyes. Flying down the steps, she finally looked out at the parking lot. And that was when she saw the last spirit bus trailing smoke and chugging away down Holiday Street. Knowing she would never make it to Eric's game, she crumpled down next to the old statue of the sea lion and began to sob.

SEVENTEEN

Kat was waiting. Her hands were like ice. Her stomach kept flipping over. She had to take a deep breath each time she checked her parents' big grandfather clock. When the clock struck eight, she froze as if she'd been put under a spell.

Rrrrffff, rrrrrrf, rrrrrrff!

"Rocket, cut that out!" Kat snapped, coming to life again. She pushed away her dog, who was snapping at her old, black flats. "I'm going to a dance. Don't slobber on me." She took a shaky breath again and held back tears. "At least I hope I'm going. I hope this last joke isn't on me."

Rocket went back to racing back and forth in front of the living-room window seat. He put his paws up, then looked out and barked at every car that passed down the street. Kat sat on the love seat next to him folding and unfolding her hands, crossing her legs, and reminding herself to swallow. She, too, was watching every car. So far none of them had been Brent's red BMW.

"What time did Brent say he was coming for you?" Kat's mom called from the dining room, where she was setting up guest tables for Sunday morning breakfast.

"Seven forty-five," Kat answered. She smoothed down her silky black skirt and didn't say anything else.

Her mom didn't push it, but kept folding napkins and humming to herself. Kat was left to look out the window and pray.

Kat prayed that Brent would show up. She prayed that Miranda had been wrong. She hadn't seen Miranda at the game the night before, and she wouldn't have spoken to her even if she had. Kat had never known Miranda to be malicious, but it couldn't possibly be true that Brent was anything but a fabulous, decent guy. It could be some kind of misunderstanding, or some twisted tenth-hand gossip. Or maybe Miranda hadn't heard anything at all. Maybe Miranda was simply confused because of what had happened to Kat last summer.

Kat sat on her hands and rocked. *She* was still confused about what happened to her last summer. She'd never told the whole truth to Miranda, because she didn't think Miranda would ever understand. And Kat had been so hurt that she hadn't wanted to admit it. That night at the old amusement park, she and Grady hadn't just ridden the roller coaster and devoured cotton candy. They'd gone back to the big vacation house he was renting with his friends. They'd joked and listened to music. They'd stayed up late. And they'd made love.

That was Kat's first and only time. Other kids at school bragged about making love, which usually made Kat sure that they were lying. Her affair with Grady wasn't something she wanted to boast about. For her it had been the opposite of jokes and wisecrack locker talk. It had been sweet and awkward and scary and very important, all of which had made it so horrible when Grady left town the next day and never called her again.

So why shouldn't she be defensive and mouthy and nervous? It was either that or let out all the stops and pay with a broken heart. If only she could have a romance that was like her friendship with Gabe . . . or like the way her friendship used to be with Gabe, minus his flirting and her cracks. That was one relationship she could think of that wouldn't leave her with a broken heart.

Now Kat had to wonder if her heart wasn't going to break again. "Brent has to show up," she whispered. "Please, please, just let him show up."

At that moment Kat's adrenaline raced, and she shot to her feet. She'd seen a flash of red speed around the corner and slow in front of her house. She clenched her fists and held her breath until she heard a car door open and saw a young man with golden hair step out. Rocket yapped, but this time Kat could have wrapped him in her arms. Brent closed the car door behind him, then strode up the brick walkway of the McDonough Bed and Breakfast, past the flowerpots and under the big magnolia tree. He shifted his shoulders in his tuxedo shirt, which was tucked into a shiny cummerbund and sleek black pants. His hair glistened under the porch light as he stepped up and rang the bell.

Kat stepped away from the window, waiting to answer so that he wouldn't think she'd doubted him. The doorbell rang again. And again. Kat's mom finally came out of the kitchen to answer, as Kat backed into the high-ceilinged hall and hid.

"Brent?"

"You must be Mrs. McDonough. Uh, is Kat here?"

"KAT, HONEY, WHERE'D YOU GO? BRENT'S HERE!"

Kat didn't move. She was still thanking her lucky stars and gathering her nerve.

"So, your house is a B and B?" Brent commented in an overly polite voice.

"Yes, it is."

"Um, so, did you go to the football game last night, Mrs. McDonough?"

"No," her mom answered, just as politely, "But Kat did. It's really too bad the team lost. Although, I still think they did remarkably well for such a small school."

Kat finally stepped down the hall and into the living room, where Brent was standing under the chandelier that shone down on the sparkly black studs running up the front of his white shirt.

As soon as he saw Kat, he smiled and held out a gold box with a silvery pink bow. "You look terrific."

Kat was flooded with relief. She took in his clear blue eyes again, his dimples, and his reassuring air. She stood very still as he walked over and produced a white orchid corsage. Kat had never pictured herself wearing a corsage, especially one as delicate and special as an orchid.

"I thought you might be wearing a strapless dress, so I asked them to put it on a wristband," Brent laughed, slipping the flower out of the box and over her hand. "Then I wondered if you might be wearing a long-sleeved dress and this might get in the way. I hope you like it."

"I love it," Kat said, already embarrassed at just how much she liked herself in the slinky black dress with the orchid on her wrist. She thought back to her funny necklace. Maybe she should run back and hang her corsage on the old string of cord, along with her nose plug and a rubber duck. But for once she was leaving her jokes at home. Brent opened the front door and gestured.

"Are you ready to go?" he asked. "Or do you want to hang around here for a few more minutes?"

Kat's mind was going blank. It wasn't only the jokes that were going; everything was fading into her relief and her pleasure at Brent's beautiful face. "Whatever you want," she mumbled.

For a second he almost seemed to frown. "Whatever I want. Okay." He smiled again. "Let's go."

"Let's go," she echoed, stepping into the warm, breezy night.

She took in Brent's gentlemanly face as they walked down to his car. No cracks this time. This evening was for real.

"TESTING THREE, TWO, ONE," Gabe said into the microphone. "Oooops, that's backwards, isn't it? Oh, well, I guess they don't call this the Turnaround Formal for nothing."

Everyone laughed. Gabe stepped off the stage while a local band named Jake and the Four Squares launched into their first set. The Ocean Star Ballroom was packed. Even though the ballroom was as big as the football field, the turnout was even bigger. There was satin rustling everywhere and glitter brushing off in little flakes. The dance committee always used a fairy-tale theme, because of the crowning of Princess and her Shining Knight. But this time it was more than construction paper cut-outs and papier-mâché moons. The Tucker Resort had obviously pitched in. There were huge painted posters in blues and pinks that looked like they were out of classic children's storybooks. A long-haired maiden riding on a horse. A knight in armor. A wicked witch. And the whole ceiling had been draped with cloth to make it look like a hundred thousand stars.

But Miranda felt anything but magical as she and Eric slow-danced. She knew they looked all right. She was in a long red dress with a flare skirt and spaghetti straps, and Eric had a matching red scarf in the pocket of his tux. They danced easily, two people who knew each other's moves. Eric never stepped on her feet, and her cheek met his shoulder at the perfect height.

What wasn't perfect was what was going on inside.

It was there again. The rolling, back and forth, queasy blurred feeling of the sand shifting out from under Miranda's feet. She was trying to hold steady.

Meanwhile, Eric was squeezing her hand as if he wanted to wring it out. He hadn't forgiven her for missing his important play-off game.

"Hi, David," Miranda managed to say, waving to David Ronkowski who appeared with Jojo only to be swallowed up by the swaying, laughing crowd again.

"Hi, Miranda! Hi, Eric! You guys look great," called Roslyn Griff.

"Good luck for Princess and her Knight," said Arnie Wheeldon, who was dancing with a girl from the gymnastics team. "You both deserve to win."

"Thanks," Miranda said.

"Thanks," Eric echoed, in his normal team captain voice. "I wouldn't mind one win this weekend," he added under his breath.

"What?" Miranda asked, pulling back and looking into Eric's sturdy face.

"I didn't say anything," he insisted, looking off at the crowd again.

"Yes, you did."

Eric kept dancing, his movements getting stiffer and more controlled with every low moan of the saxophone.

"Eric, I said I'm sorry." Miranda kept up her public smile. "I explained that I got into an argument with Kat. I lost track of time. My father already yelled at me about missing your game; you don't have to give me the cold shoulder, too."

"Just do me a favor," he muttered, still smiling for the crowd and refusing to look at her. "Don't talk about this now. If we're going to win, we'd better look like we're having a good time. I've had enough disappointment this weekend."

What about me? Miranda wanted to yell. I may have lost my best friend, or set her up to walk into some horrible trap! I've only seen Kat once tonight, when Kat first walked in with Brent. Kat looked incredibly happy, but she isn't talking to me, either, so how do I really know?

"I don't care if we win or not, Eric," Miranda blurted out.

"Miranda." He squeezed her hand more tightly.

She finally pulled her hand away and stepped back, almost knocking into Cheryl Waite and Stuart Marconi. "Look, Eric," she said in a louder voice, "I'm sorry you lost your game. I'm really sorry I didn't make it. But there's nothing I can do about it now."

The only change on Eric's face was a slight narrowing of his eyes and a tightening of his mouth. Then he broadened his Knight in Shining Armor smile again as he pulled her in to resume dancing, controlling her with his arm. "Would you do me a favor?" he ordered. "Just keep dancing and don't say another word. I'd like something this weekend to turn out right."

"Fine." Miranda stared straight ahead as couples swirled and swung around her. And as they looked at her and Eric with envy, Miranda knew what they were thinking. Most likely to succeed as Princess and her Shining Knight. Miss Perfect. Mr. Football. Couple of the Year.

"Is this band hot?"

"YESSSSSS!" the crowd roared back.

"Is this dance unforgettable?"

"YEAHHHHH!!"

Gabe did a tap dance onstage and then whistled into the mike. "Okay, Sea Lions. You're all pretty unforgettable, too. Now Jake and his buddies are going to play one more set, then we'll have a break for refreshments, thoughfully provided by the Tucker Resort. After that comes the crowning of Princess and her Knight in Shininnng Armoooor. Our committee is deciding the winners right now, so keep your fingers crossed."

More applause and cheers. Gabe grinned. Up onstage in front of his classmates not only was he safe from romance, but he could look out over the crowd and survey his friends. Miranda and Eric looked great in their matching red, although something was definitely missing. They danced like two A students in dancing class, not like two people who were wildly in love. Of course, Gabe had always had that impression of Miranda and Eric, so it wasn't a big surprise.

Jojo looked like an electric Christmas tree in a green dress and green shoes. Her hair was laced with tiny sparkler things that Gabe couldn't quite figure out. By contrast her date, David, was one of those guys who did not look comfortable in a tux. That was okay, because Jojo seemed to be having a great time. She was flitting like a butterfly back and forth between different groups of kids.

Gabe looked around some more. He spotted Lisa Avery, wearing a fabulously low-cut gown and leading around a college guy that she looked bored with already. Meanwhile, off in the corner, Gabe spotted Jackson Magruder. He was as inconspicuous as Lisa was flashy. Jackson was attending the dance solo and certainly hadn't bothered with a tux. Of course, neither had Gabe, since he couldn't afford to rent one. He'd worn his regular black jeans and T-shirt with a tuxedo jacket borrowed from the drama department at school.

Gabe caught Jackson's eye and raised a hand in greeting from the stage. Jackson nodded.

Gabe drew in a breath. There was one more person he should look for in the crowd, but he was almost afraid he'd find her. But try as he might, he couldn't keep his eyes away. Kat. She was wearing a knockout black dress that set off her strong swimmer's shoulders and beautiful, slender back. It was the kind of dress that made you notice the way Kat's hair curled right at the nape of her neck.

Unfortunately, the pleasure of seeing Kat look so gorgeous was spoiled by the sight of Brent Tucker standing next to her. He was holding his punch cup and smiling in a way that made Gabe think he was a little bit bored.

"Why does that guy bug me all of a sudden?" Gabe had to ask himself as he stepped down from the stage and grabbed a cup from a table decorated with silver stars. "And how could any guy be bored with Kat?"

Everybody thought Brent was the greatest thing since Christmas vacation, but as Gabe watched Brent lead Kat onto the dance floor, Gabe just couldn't agree. Something about Brent's crisp, preppy ease was starting to make Gabe's skin crawl. Maybe it was seeing Kat act so demure and unKatlike around him. Gabe couldn't stop staring until someone nudged him.

It was David Ronkowski. "Where's Chip?" David asked.

"He decided not to come," Gabe answered.

"Too bad." David noticed that Gabe was watching Kat again. "Kat and that Tucker guy make quite a couple. I think they have a chance at Princess and her Knight." He shrugged. "I know Jojo'd like to win, too, but I don't think I'm exactly knight material."

"Who is?" Gabe tossed back, looking over at Miranda and Eric again.

David laughed as if he didn't quite get the joke, then lifted two cups of punch and started to make his way back through the crowd. "See you," he said.

Gabe didn't respond. He was too preoccupied with staring at Kat and Brent.

"So who do you really think will win?" Jojo wondered out loud.

She was surrounded by a host of admirers: Shelley Lara, Bill Johnson, Dawn Chapwin, and Ian Holme. They were looking down at the ocean view together, while the band went into their last number of the set, an incredibly fast country jig that no one in their right mind could move to. Jojo had been enjoying the dance a lot more than she thought she would, especially considering the run-in with Leanne and last night's depressing football game. Her green dress and green shoes were a hit. David hadn't turned out to be such a dud, even though Jojo had been worried at first when he'd tried to pin on her corsage and had just about drawn blood.

"I think it's a close contest," Bill Johnson answered, hunching his tall, broad shoulders and putting his arm around Shelley, who kept glancing back to Gabe.

"Can you count Lisa Avery and Roslyn Griff, since they're both here with guys who don't go to Crescent?" Shelley asked.

"I don't know," Jojo admitted. She spotted David weaving through the crowd carrying two cups of punch. She waved him over.

"What about you and your gang?" asked Dawn, a horsy type who wanted to be a vet.

"Miranda's always a possibility for anything," Shelley agreed. "But maybe Kat will win, since she's with Brent." She smiled at Jojo. "Maybe all three of you will tie."

Jojo would have liked that. She would have liked anything that might have linked her with Miranda and Kat. Even though neither girl was mad at her, Jojo could tell that they were keeping to their respective corners like boxers in a prize fight.

Miranda and Kat had both called her that day, which was weird because they usually talked to each other, and censored the juicy stuff when it came to her. Miranda had wanted to know where Jojo's info about Brent had come from. Kat had wanted to know who could have said something to Miranda about Brent. For once Jojo hadn't breathed a word, even though she'd begun to wonder if what Leanne told her had really been the truth. She'd also wondered if she'd started some huge rift between Kat and Miranda that could hang on and hurt them all.

"I guess we'll just have to wait and find out," Jojo said.

The foursome nodded and moved away to meet David, as he squeezed away from the dance floor and handed Jojo some punch. Jojo sipped and smiled at him and thought about Miranda and Kat. She could socialize; she could dance her brains out; she could smile and gossip and shop, but none of it meant a thing if her real friends were falling apart.

"Do you mind if I go to the powder room for the refreshment break?" she asked David, giving him back her punch cup. "I'll be back for the crowning of Princess and her Knight."

David shrugged. "Okay," he said cheerfully, heading over to join Shelley, Bill, Ian, and Dawn. "Don't be too long."

Jojo nodded and headed into the crowd, most of whom had given up dancing and were mingling and talking in very loud voices. She passed Lisa, but didn't even stop to say hello. Instead, she went straight for Kat, who was standing near the refreshment table, watching the waiters set it up. Every so often she gazed admiringly at Brent.

Jojo tugged Kat's hand. "Will you meet me in the ladies' room after this song? The one off the lobby, near that outdoor elevator."

With a touch of alarm, Kat looked at Brent. "Is that okay with you?"

"I don't mind," Brent said.

"Are you sure? You really don't mind?"

Brent sighed. "I really don't mind, Kat."

Kat looked back at Jojo, then nodded.

Mission accomplished. Jojo traipsed, wove, and excuse-me'd her way over to the other side of the room, where Miranda was standing next to Eric. Both of them were looking off in different directions. Their pose kind of reminded Jojo of arctic explorers. In fact, if Eric's cummerbund hadn't matched Miranda's dress, a stranger might not have know they were a couple.

But Miranda perked up when she saw Jojo.

"Meet me in five minutes in the bathroom off the lobby, the one by the outdoor elevator," Jojo told her.

Miranda nodded gratefully, as if she were glad for any excuse to get away.

Jojo waved and smiled her way through the crowd again, heading for the bathroom so that she could get there first and figure out how to reconcile Miranda and Kat. She wanted their old trio to be a unit again. And she also wanted them to be together, just in case there was some unexpected competition for Princess and her Shining Knight.

EIGHTEEN

"Great place, Brent."

"Brent, this is wonderful."

"Good luck for Shining Knight. You deserve it, man."

"Please say thank-you to your folks, Brent."

Brent accepted the back slapping, the handshaking, the smiles, and acknowledgments with easy graciousness. He flirted with the girls who flirted with him first, basked in the attention of the big guys — the seniors, the football jocks, the student body officers, and anybody else who looked like he was cool.

But underneath it all Brent was going crazy with restlessness. The effort of all his politeness and charm was making him feel like he was going to shoot through the roof.

"Hey, Brent. Do you think we could have the dance here again next year?"

"Brent, the food is incredible."

"This is the best dance ever, Brent. Thank you so much."

Brent continued padding across the ballroom, offering soft thank-yous while squeezing through the crowd. He wanted to get far away from the spot where Kat had left him and take as long a breather as he could. He'd been relieved when she'd gone off with her cheerleader friend. Not that Kat was such a horrendous bore, but she was too easily fooled, too willing to accept the person he was trying to put over. The quirky humor he'd seen in her at school had been replaced by wimpy politeness. If she asked him one more time if something was okay with him, he was going to lose his mind. If only she'd tripped him up once or twice, stood up to him, or told him off, he might actually have gone for her.

Still, he couldn't afford to alienate Kat or her important friends. If he was going to be stuck in Crescent Bay — and it looked like he was — he would need allies. Kat and her friends were important.

Brent took a shortcut behind the bandstand,

where the guitars rested against their stands, and half-filled glasses of watery soda sat on amplifiers. That was another thing he had to get away from. The band. He hadn't fine-tuned his ears with the most expensive audio equipment, and best recorded classical CD's, only to be assaulted by the twangy sound of Jake and the Four Squares.

Brent headed for the door, wondering how long he could afford to be away. He'd sensed that Kat and the cheerleader weren't going off simply to redo their lipstick. He'd seen that look on Kat's friend's face, the let's-get-together-and-tell-each-other-everything-that's-happened-at-this-dance-so-far look. Kat would be gone for ten minutes at least. And surely she'd be back in time for the announcement of Princess and her Shining Knight. That was okay. Ten minutes was long enough for him to sneak over to the kitchen and see what he could do.

Brent knew Leanne was working that night. He pictured her standing over steaming dish machines with her Madonna hair, while the rest of them danced in prom clothes and ate little rolls filled up with crab. The contrast made him want to howl with laughter. He still remembered the feel of his body pressed against her and ached to feel that way again. He decided right then and there that it was definitely time to pay Leanne another visit.

But before Brent could make it out the ball-room door, someone grabbed the back of his tux jacket with ferocious energy. Before he quite knew what had happened, he'd been pulled out of the entrance traffic, and back into the ballroom crowd.

"Where are you going in such a hurry?" the girl asked, her eyes looking right into his.

"Who wants to know?" he tossed back.

She had flaming red hair and a pink mouth that was slick with lip gloss. Her dress was short and scoop-necked and almost looked as if it were made of foil. Her figure was pure Barbie Doll — not lush and real like Leanne's, but tempting nonetheless. She met his eye with incredible directness, something that no girl had done since Brent had started Crescent Bay High. Even a powerhouse like Miranda Jamison had been a little intimidated by his slickness and his looks.

She stuck out her hand. "I'm Lisa Avery, and I've been wanting to meet you," she said without a hint of coyness.

He shook her hand. She didn't let his hand go. "I'm Brent Tucker."

"As if I didn't know."

They stared at one another until they both relaxed into sly smiles.

"My date went to the can," Brent hinted.

"Mine went outside to have a smoke," she answered right away.

"Sounds like an opportunity."

"And you know what they say. If you pass up an opportunity, it may never come again."

Brent was enjoying this. It was like something he would have initiated, and it was nervy as all get-out. To everyone standing nearby, it must have looked as if he and Lisa were having the standard Turnaround dance conversation. *Thank your parents, Brent. Do you really live right here in the resort? Can you arrange to play golf whenever you want and swim in all the pools?* In reality they were arranging something much more tantalizing.

"Where?" she demanded.

"Just outside the first-floor suites. There's an alcove there with an ice machine. Ask the concierge the way to suite 112."

She smiled. "When?"

"There's no time like the present."

"So nice talking to you."

"See you around," he said, taking the opposite route to reach their destination.

When Brent walked away, his step had taken on new life.

The powder room off the main lobby had black-and-white floors, marble sinks with faucets shaped like shells, and bouquets of apricot-colored silk flowers. When Miranda first went in she didn't see anyone. Unlike the ladies' room adjoining the ballroom — which was a madhouse of spritzing and smudging — in this restroom there was no sound other that faint Muzak and the *tap, tap* of a drippy faucet.

Miranda stood for a moment staring into the mirror. She still looked like the old, intense Miranda. The glossy red ribbon was still woven into the side of her hair, and her blue eyes still looked full of smarts and purpose. But just when she thought she was looking okay, Miranda had to hunch over and hold onto the side of the sink. With every dance, every compliment, every wish of luck for Princess and her Knight, Eric's silence had become more and more oppressive. It was like dancing with a mannequin. Eric kept up his frozen smile for the adoring public, but he was all hollow inside when it came to her.

Miranda turned on the shell faucet, letting cold water dribble over her hands until she brought the coolness to her face. She knew that Eric was hurt and disappointed, but she was hurt and disappointed, too. For once she couldn't ignore it.

A moment later, Miranda heard bubbly laughter as the outside door was opened and two girls burst in. She'd expected Jojo. When she saw Kat come through the swinging inner door as well, she felt the pull of tears.

"Miranda, you beat us here," Jojo said with a funny expression, not looking back at Kat. "I couldn't quite remember where this bathroom was. I wanted us to meet someplace where there weren't a hundred other people."

Good old Jojo, Miranda thought. She tried to connect with Kat's eyes, but Kat still wouldn't quite look at her. When Jojo planted herself in front of the mirror and emptied makeup from a small, sequined purse, Miranda and Kat fell in on either side. Between Jojo's sparkly green, her solid red, and Kat's elegant black, they looked like a foreign flag.

"Okay. I did this on purpose," Jojo admitted as she swept blusher up her cheek. "Don't be mad at me. I did it for a good cause. I'm into good causes lately to make up for the damage I do the rest of the time."

Miranda wanted to throw her arms around Jojo. She wanted to throw her arms around Kat, too. She wanted to sit on the cold tile with her two old friends and not leave the bathroom until the dance was completely done.

"Hi," Miranda said to Kat, trying to catch her eye in the mirror.

Kat fiddled with her bangs. "Hi," she finally responded.

"It looks like you're having a great time with Brent. I'm glad."

Kat nodded. "Pretty good," she said in a cool voice. "Yeah. Really good, actually." She borrowed Jojo's blusher.

"I guess I was wrong," Miranda admitted. She had regretted warning Kat about Brent, but now she was having doubts again. As the dance had worn on, Miranda had kept her eye on Brent. She'd started to get an eerie feeling, but she didn't know how to put it. "I'm sorry," was the best she could do for now.

Kat handed back the cosmetic brush and played with the corsage on her wrist. Jojo continued to pat and dab. "How about you?" Kat asked coolly. "Are you and Eric having a good time? Are you going to be king and queen, the grand pooh-bahs of the dance?"

Miranda flinched. "Eric's still mad about my missing his game. Maybe he's just mad about losing. We'll work it out." Even as she said it, she realized that she might not want to work it out. Part of her never wanted to look at Eric's face again.

"Well, I'm having a good time with David," Jojo volunteered. "Not that it's any big infatuation or anything. I mean, I'm not getting *those feelings*. But he's a good guy, and he's pretty fun to have as a date."

"Good," Kat said.

"Good," Miranda echoed.

Then the three of them stood looking in the mirror rubbing away smudges of mascara and examining their gowns.

When a few more minutes had passed, Jojo spoke up. "We'd better go back. They're announcing Princess and her Knight. I'll arrange more of these three-party meeting sessions later. Don't worry."

"I'm not worried."

"We never worry about you, Jojo."

"Let's go."

Miranda led the way, with Kat and Jojo following. It wasn't until they were all the way down the first-floor hall that Miranda realized she'd gone in the wrong direction again. She was starting to feel like she could walk outside and step into the resort swimming pool without even realizing it.

"Is this the right way?" Kat asked.

"It had better be," said Jojo. "I don't want to miss Princess and her Knight."

They went down the hall with cool green carpet and walls with paisley trim. They turned a corner past an abandoned metal cart stacked with dirty dishes and an empty bottle of champagne. Miranda heard the humming and clunking of a nearby ice machine and then heard something else that seemed so out of context that she had to stop and stare.

"Brent, we'd better get back," she heard a girl giggle.

"We will, Lisa. We will."

Miranda knew instantly. She turned around to at least stop Kat from seeing, but it was too late. Miranda watched Kat's mouth go slack, and her eyes glaze over. The three of them stood staring at Brent and Lisa, standing in a small alcove, necking and groping as if they were going for a world record.

Jojo gasped.

Kat put her hand to her mouth, as if she might throw up.

Brent finally heard them and pulled back, but Lisa just grinned. Her pink gooey lipstick was all over Brent's face and one strap of her dress had fallen down. She yanked it up as she eyed the three girls.

"Oops," Lisa said, grinning. Then she put a finger to her lips in an exaggerated *shhhhh*. She let out one more giggle, waved to Brent, and tiptoed away.

The worst thing about the whole discovery was the sudden flash of arrogance Miranda suddenly saw in Brent's deep blue eyes. He flicked hair away from his face and the flash quickly disappeared, replaced by an oily smoothness.

"Kat, oh, man." Brent sighed painfully. "What a mess. That girl is nuts. Let me explain. . . ."

Kat didn't let him explain anything. She let out a horrible moan, turned around, and ran straight back to the bathroom, immediately followed by Miranda and Jojo.

Within seconds the three of them were surrounded by black-and-white tile again, and Kat began to sob. Her body shuddered. She wailed and trembled as if the pain were coming from the bottom of her feet. Jojo had gone pale under her makeup, and Miranda was crying, too.

Miranda tried to hug Kat, but Kat pushed her away as her tears kept pouring down. "Just go back to the dance!" Kat cried out. "Go win everything and do everything, but just do it for yourself this time, and don't pretend that any of it is for me. Don't ever do anything for me again!"

"Look," Jojo said in desperation. "Maybe it was Lisa's fault. You know what she's like."

Kat cried harder.

"Kat," Miranda said. "Maybe Jojo's right."

Kat put her hands to her face again as if she didn't even want to look at Miranda. "Go back to Eric. Leave me alone. You've done enough damage. JUST LEAVE ME ALONE!"

Miranda backed her way out of the bathroom and into the hall. Kat's sobbing filled her head, and she couldn't think of anything else. She wandered through the lobby, past the potted trees and the resort employees in their uniforms, across a dining room and by a kitchen where the food smell almost made her sick. Finally she saw a sign pointing the way to the Ocean Star Ballroom.

There was a bottleneck at the ballroom's entrance and everyone was looking toward the stage where Gabe was handing over the floor to president Roslyn Griff. The crowd quieted as Roslyn stepped up to the mike. "Hello, Sea Lions," she said in a warm voice. "I know that everyone is waiting for my announcement, but first I'd like to extend a big thank-you. Let's all hear it for Brent Tucker and the Tucker Resort! Is this the best formal dance we've ever had at Crescent Bay High?"

The cheers and hollers of approval turned Miranda's stomach.

"Where is Brent?" Roslyn asked, putting a hand to her face as she leaned into the stage light. "Brent? Can you show yourself and take a bow?"

Brent was onstage instantly. Miranda didn't see any trace of Lisa's lipstick as he took a modest bow.

More applause and cheers.

"Okay, I won't torture you any longer," Roslyn said with a big smile. She ripped open the envelope, which took some fiddling because of her long satin gloves. Finally she plucked out the sheet of paper. "The winning couple for this year's Princess and her Shining Knight are . . . "

The crowd became completely still.

"MIRANDA JAMISON AND ERIC GERACI!"

Miranda saw the crowd begin to part around Eric, who was moving toward the stage, keeping up his smile, while desperately looking around.

Miranda tried to make herself walk into the ballroom. She knew she had to do it. She planned to do it. She told herself it was the right, the only thing to do.

But she couldn't. The sand had washed away. Her world had fallen in. There was only one thing to do.

Run.

Leanne wasn't sure she wanted to take a break.

Outside the kitchen the Princess and her Knight coronation was still going on. Meanwhile she was wearing jeans, a secondhand man's shirt, black Chinese slippers, and a stained white apron. Her hair was pulled back into a bun, and she'd burned herself twice that night grabbing dishes before they'd had a chance to cool. This was not a night when she was in a mood to compare outfits with her classmates.

But she also wanted to get away from the

smell of soapsuds and old soup. That decided, she wiped her red hands on her apron, then untied it. "I'm on break," she yelled to the cook, on the other side of the kitchen. He gave her the okay, and she headed toward the small outdoor deck where employees ate their meals. On the way, she made a cup of tea at the waiters' station.

It was still fairly warm, and from the deck Leanne could hear the tumble of the waves. She sat very still for a few minutes, just listening to the ocean and breathing in the steam from the tea and the salty air.

Leanne heard someone else come out onto the deck, but didn't look up. She hadn't been very friendly with the other kitchen workers, and she was in no mood to change that now. But as she still sat quietly sipping, a girl in a long black dress walked slowly past her until she reached the railing and collapsed against it. The girl's bare shoulders caved in and her back trembled as she looked out over the sea.

Leanne knew it was someone from the dance, but it took her some time to recognize Kat McDonough, Jojo's friend. The first thing that shot through Leanne's mind was that she'd been discovered in the kitchen. Jojo had somehow found this out, too, and sent Kat to gloat, or dig up even more dirt.

But then Kat turned around. Even under the dim deck light, Leanne could tell that Kat had been crying. Her eyes were puffy and even her mouth looked raw.

"Can I stand out here for a few minutes?" Kat whispered.

Leanne wasn't sure if Kat remembered who she was. "Why not?"

Kat looked out at the water again, then put her face into her hands. After a few minutes she turned back, as if she were trying to get herself to leave the deck and walk back in. Eventually her swollen eyes focused on Leanne. "You're Leanne, right?" she finally mumbled, taking in Leanne's grubby clothes.

Leanne steeled herself. Maybe she'd been wrong about the tears. Maybe this was a mission from Jojo after all.

"What are you doing here?" Kat asked in a weak voice.

Leanne stood up. "Look, if you want to know more about where I live, and why I'm working here, just tell your friend Jojo to hire a detective."

Kat's body crumpled a little. She shook her head.

Leanne noticed Kat's wounded eyes again and remembered Brent. She wondered if Jojo had passed on her warning. At the same time, she had the very clear sense that Kat didn't know what she was talking about.

Kat started to move away from the railing and began to drift back across the deck.

"Isn't Brent Tucker your date tonight?" Leanne suddenly asked.

"Why?"

"Forget it," Leanne backtracked, still looking at Kat's eyes for some kind of connection, some recognition that Jojo had told all. But all she saw was more of Kat's private grief and pain.

Kat took a shaky breath. "It doesn't matter. I came to the dance with Brent. But I don't think I'm leaving with him." A tiny sob came up, but she tried to hold it back.

Leanne stepped forward, moved by the deep humiliation in Kat's voice. She doubted that Brent would have the nerve to treat Kat the way he'd treated her, but she sensed that she and Kat had shared some of the same humiliation nonetheless. Kat started toward the door, almost as if she were moving in slow motion.

For some reason, Leanne had to stop her. She needed to make some kind of connection, some link besides her own secret knowledge that they had both been hurt by the same sleazy boy. "Don't let him get to you," she said with real conviction.

Kat turned back with a stunned expression. "What?"

Leanne looked right at her. "It's none of my business, but if I were you, there's one thing I'd do before I went back into the ballroom."

"Who says I'm going back?" Kat shuddered, wiping her eyes with the back of her arm.

"Go back," Leanne advised, remembering all the times that she'd run away. She picked up her teacup and walked past Kat, stopping to lightly touch Kat's bare arm. "You have to go back. Just wash your face before you face all your friends. Take it from me, nothing's worse than letting them all see you cry."

NINETEEN

"Lisa is crazy, Kat. I'm new here. I didn't know what I was getting into when she found me in that hall. I was just wandering around trying to find you."

Brent was shifting smoothly, gearing down in the BMW as he drove Kat home. He was talking smoothly, too. Kat sat with her hands locked together, and her eyes staring blankly. She wondered if he thought he'd gotten away with it, just because she hadn't run into Ocean Star Ballroom, raving to everyone that he was a liar and a slime.

"I mean, what kind of girl leaves her date alone at a dance and goes after someone else?" Brent asked as he pulled up in front of her house.

A question I might ask you, Kat wanted to scream. But she didn't say a word. She sat very still, holding onto her dignity with the little bit of strength she had left. Something about Leanne's advice had gotten to her. She'd at least managed to get herself back into the dance and to allow Brent to drive her home. But the tears still pressed at the back of her throat, and her hands still trembled. She didn't know how long she could hold on.

"I'm sorry," Brent said, shaking his head and turning off the engine. They sat in the car while a pair of guests strolled up the brick walkway and into Kat's house. "What was I supposed to do? Push her away? I didn't know what to do. She caught me totally off guard."

Kat ran the whole nightmare over in her head. After leaving Leanne, she'd gone back and tried to wash her face, but it was hopeless. That kind of humiliation didn't wash away so easily. When she'd gone back to the ballroom, she'd still looked puffy and wiped out, but with all the commotion about Miranda, no one would have noticed if she'd gone off and shaved her head. Kat had finally found Brent and begged, "Let's go. I'd really like you to take me home right now." And that was the only thing she'd said to him before their short ride back to her house.

Brent leaned forward and ran a hand through his golden hair. His tux jacket had been thrown onto the backseat, and he'd unbuttoned the top two studs of his shirt. Kat's corsage had begun to wilt. "Pretty weird how your friend just left Eric Geraci to win that Shining Knight thing with no Princess. I bet he didn't feel like a shining knight." Brent tapped the steering wheel with his knuckles. "What a mind-blower. You never know about those uptight, do-everything types. I guess something had to give."

As angry as she still was at Miranda, Kat hated hearing Brent talking about her. On top of everything, Kat was horribly worried about her best friend. She'd heard the outraged gossip start as soon as people had realized what was going on. Brent was wrong. Ditching Eric for the crowning wasn't just something that had to give. It was Miranda tossing away everything she'd ever worked for.

Brent put a classical tape into the tape deck, and Kat thought longingly of her friends. She thought of Jojo trying so hard to bring them back together. Just before leaving the dance, Jojo had even promised not to tell anyone about seeing Brent and Lisa. Kat hadn't asked it of her, although she was grateful nonetheless. She pictured Chip's sweet face and wondered why no girl had thought to ask him to the dance. And she thought of Gabe, who she'd caught staring at her from up onstage. She'd stared back at him, which had only made him look away.

Brent turned in his seat and faced her, his discomfort turning into shame. "Anyway, I don't know what else to say to you, Kat. I know I sound like a jerk, and actually, well, I pretty much feel like a jerk."

Kat looked at him again, and for the first time since she had caught him with Lisa, she was startled to remember what she'd seen in him. She took in the refined line of his brow, his perfectly straight nose, and strong, elegant mouth. He smiled sadly, and his dimples made him look even more gentlemanly and innocent. "You *are* a jerk," she managed to say.

Brent nodded, then he tried to smile. "Kat, can't you imagine yourself doing something like what I did tonight?"

Kat flinched.

"I'm not trying to insult you," he argued. "I mean it honestly. I admit, I could have gotten away from Lisa if I'd really wanted to. But she came on so strong, and I guess I thought it was a lark. It didn't mean anything. It's only the first date between you and me, so it isn't like there's some heavy commitment between us. Come on,

Kat. Lisa's gorgeous. And she's really nervy. Most guys would have done exactly what I did. They just might not have been dumb enough to get caught. Tell me honestly, haven't you ever lost your head and done something you regretted?"

Kat's heart jolted. She looked down at her hands while the breeze rustled the leaves of a nearby tree. "Good night," she said, reaching for the door.

"Haven't you?" he repeated. "If the answer is no, then you don't have to forgive me. But if the answer is yes, then I think you have to forgive me just a little."

Kat didn't move.

"Thanks for asking me to this," he said gently, scooping up her hand and cradling it in his.

Kat felt herself losing ground.

"In spite of everything, I had a great time with you."

"Sure."

"I did."

She felt like she was going to cry again.

Then he was gently pulling her toward him while turning and leaning in his seat to meet her. With tenderness he took her hand and pressed it to his face. Kat felt the warm softness of his lean cheek. He closed his eyes, then he pressed his lips to hers.

Kat told herself to be as responsive as a piece of wood. But the minute she felt his hand creep up her back, his mouth on hers, his silky hair against her face, she started to feel loose-limbed and dizzy. She leaned into him and initiated a second kiss, which lasted even longer than the first. Only when she was breathless and disoriented, did she separate from him and push away.

"Please don't walk me to the door," she managed before she climbed out.

"Wait a minute," Brent protested, lunging over the seat and reaching out to her. "I want to see you again. Can I call you?"

Kat backed up. She was afraid to take his hand or get too close to the car again. "You can call me next week . . . but I don't know what's going to happen," she answered.

"Who does?" Brent responded, offering a satisfied smile. "I'll take my chances."

"Okay," Kat breathed. She took a few steps backwards, still staring at him sprawled across his car seat, until she walked into a flowerpot and heard the hollow crack as it fell over and broke. Her heart was still racing as she kicked the broken pottery aside and ran up the pathway to her house.

Miranda had raced out of the resort lobby, flying like a crazy person. When she ran into the parking lot, she thought she was completely alone. But she was surprised. Someone had followed her.

"Jackson."

"I ran down here as soon as I saw what was going on," he'd said to Miranda. "I'm so glad I caught you."

"I won't go back in there," Miranda had cried. "I won't go! Don't try and make me."

"I won't make you go back. You don't have to go back."

"I just want to get out of here."

Jackson had nodded. "Okay. Just let me come with you."

And so they'd begun to run. She'd hiked up her red dress and moved like lightning, through the resort parking lot, and on from there. Knowing that Jackson was at her side, she'd crossed the promenade and leaped onto the beach, stumbling when she hit the dry sand.

Jackson had thrown off his shoes, so she'd kicked off her shoes that had been dyed to match her dress and left them behind, too. Then she'd run and run until she didn't think her legs could fight the heavy sand any longer. Jackson had kept up with her until they had both dropped onto the beach, panting, legs entangled, about twenty feet from shore.

That was where they'd been ever since. There was no one else around. The waves broke softly as Miranda began to really think about what she'd done.

"Poor Eric," she gasped.

"It's okay," Jackson assured her.

"It's not okay. What I did was terrible. I'm not the kind of person who does something like that."

"Miranda, it's over," Jackson soothed. "You did what you had to do."

She began to cry again. But this time she didn't resist Jackson's arms. She reached for him, and sobbing, she clung to him. She felt his arms around her, and his cheek pressed hard against hers. There was no more holding back, no room for thinking or worrying how this was going to turn out. She just wept until she couldn't weep anymore. Finally she collapsed against him, feeling completely drained.

"What am I going to do now?" she whispered.

"I don't know."

"How will I ever show my face again at school?"

"You will, Miranda. You will."

"How?"

He ran his hand through her hair, and she nestled her face against his warm, bare neck. "When you're not prepared for it, it really kicks you in the head, doesn't it?"

Miranda pulled back to look at him. She took in every corner of Jackson's moonlit face. His curious green eyes looked like they were trying to read her every thought. His hair was being tossed by the ocean wind. His crooked smile had been replaced by an expression that was much more tender, something that made her think of love.

Miranda suddenly wondered if what she was starting to feel for Jackson might have to do with love. All she knew was that she'd never planned to be with him on the beach. But she hadn't loved Eric, in spite of all her plans. Now she wanted to feel something that was unplanned and real.

Jackson was still gazing at her. Slowly he touched her naked shoulders, his fingers running down her arms as if he were curious about the texture of her bare skin. She began to feel dizzy as she leaned forward, then stopped, his mouth so close to hers, his gaze turning even softer and more gentle. One side of his mouth turned up in a tiny, unbelieving smile. She smiled, too.

They kissed a slow, soft, open-mouthed kiss that made Miranda feel faint. Then he knelt, facing her on the sand. He ran his hands over her bare shoulders, and she reached for him, her hands sliding under his sweater, up his bare back. He kissed the hollow of her neck. She kissed his cheek, his chin, his ear, tasting a hint of salt. As if by unspoken agreement, she stretched out on the sand, and he stretched out beside her. Her legs, bare under her formal dress, felt the cool sand shift beneath her. Then she felt his heart beating within his chest, as she moved close, entwining her legs with his and feeling the warmth of his hands on her shoulders and her back.

She wasn't sure how long they lay there kissing, breathing hard, and holding each other. They could have lain on the beach all night. It turned into one big circle of motion and need — of warm skin and soft lips, of closeness and touch. All Miranda knew was that it was long enough for her to become a new person, because the old Miranda, with all the old names, could never have felt like this.

Jackson was finally the one to pull back. In the middle of a kiss he suddenly sat up. "This is scary," he admitted in a shaky voice. "Even for me."

For some reason, Miranda wasn't scared at all. Not anymore.

They sat and watched the water for a while, until Jackson stood up and offered his hands. She finally found her feet. Her dress was hiked up, totally lopsided. Sand stuck to her skin.

"It's late," Jackson said, "Maybe we'd better get you home. My folks are probably worrying about me, too."

For the first time that evening Miranda remembered home. She thought about her father, and her limbs froze up like ice. Clinging close, she and Jackson walked back up the sand and down the dark prom until they came to her house, the one brightly lit glass-and-wooden box in an otherwise moonlit night.

Right away, Miranda saw her father waiting for her, pacing the kitchen in his sweatsuit, a coffee mug in his hand. Even though she knew he might see her, she threw herself at Jackson and kissed him one last time.

"I'll talk to you tomorrow," he said, holding her so hard she could barely breathe.

She sensed that he wanted to say something else and held onto his hands until she knew she had to go in. Finally she let him go and walked up the gravel path to where her father was waiting on the other side of the door.

As soon as she walked up the deck, she remembered that her dress was dotted with sand and so were her arms and legs. She was barefoot. There was even sand tangled up in the little piece of red ribbon in her hair.

Her father opened the door before she reached him. He looked tense and angry as he peered past her. Jackson was still standing there. Her father pulled her inside the kitchen and slammed the door.

"Who was that?" he demanded.

"A friend from school."

"The skateboard kid?"

Miranda didn't answer. She recognized a trembly tightness around his mouth that meant there was no point in trying to reason or get through.

"Do you know what time it is?" he asked.

She shook her head.

"It's after two in the morning. Where've you been?"

She stared at the floor.

"I already knew you weren't with Eric because he came by here. He told us what you did."

Miranda thought of her and Jackson on the beach and wondered how Eric could have known about that. But then she realized that her father was talking about what she did to Eric at the dance. She noticed her father staring at her dress.

"I'm too angry and disappointed in you to talk about this," her father raved. "I want you upstairs right now. You'll face your mother and me in the morning. And whoever that boy is, I don't ever want to see him again."

Gathering her sandy skirt around her knees, Miranda walked past her father and climbed the wooden stairs.

TWENTY

The renovation of the Crescent Bay High quad began first thing Monday morning. While the students yawned and tried to keep their eyes open through first period physics and English classes, a back hoe rumbled just outside their windows, digging up the patchy grass to replace it with a brand-new lawn.

But even after all their hard fund-raising work, no one in the junior class was taking much interest in the new quad. No one commented on the temporary wire fence or the funny-looking slabs of sod. It seemed as if even the premature end of the football season had been forgotten. Instead they were all gossiping about Miranda.

"She could at least have left him a note."

"It makes me sick. She had everything any girl could ever want, and she threw it all away."

"And to do that to a guy like Eric Geraci, especially after he'd just lost that big game."

"It's so cruel."

"It's so low."

"I always told you she didn't really care."

By lunchtime, Kat had heard so much of that kind of talk that she wanted to bash her classmates' heads together. She didn't know what had happened Saturday night, but she knew Miranda. Miranda might push and plan, but she would never desert someone without a good reason. And whatever Miranda's reason had been, she'd paid dearly for it. On Sunday, Kat and Jojo had gone to Miranda's house, only to be told that Miranda was grounded with a capital G. No phone calls. No visitors. No going out at all, except for school.

Kat needed to talk to Miranda, so she'd looked for her at school all morning. She'd finally spotted her between second and third periods, just before the tardy bell. They'd passed one another quickly in the hall, and Miranda had looked at Kat with wild, confused eyes. Kat still felt wild and confused, too, about Brent and how Miranda had set her up. But that look in Miranda's eyes made Kat forgive a lot.

Kat was still looking for Miranda as the junior class scattered and kept up their gossip and munched. Kat checked the quad, which smelled of fertilizer. She checked Jojo's locker, but no one was there yet. She checked the library and the student council room, then began to wander aimlessly until she neared the radio station.

Gabe was standing in the doorway to the audiovisual room, staring into space, then jotting things down on a pad, as if he were working on that week's playlist. When he saw Kat he tipped the pencil to his forehead in a mock salute.

"You alone?" Kat asked. For some reason it felt strange to see Gabe again.

"Of course I'm alone," Gabe barked. His curly hair was a little unruly, and he wore his standard colored T-shirt and black jeans. He stuck his pencil behind his ear. "What do you think, I invite my entire Spanish class to come into the radio station and watch me think?"

Kat played with her woven necklace, from which she'd dangled a felt-tip pen, a Gumby eraser, and a button that read, *So I'm a fool, you fool*. "I don't know. I thought maybe one of your adoring girls might be in there waiting for you."

"Nah." He looked away. "I had enough adoration watching you and that Brent at the bizarre dance."

Kat suddenly realized that, with the exception

of Jojo, Miranda, and Lisa, of course, no one knew what had really happened between her and Brent. She still wasn't sure what had really happened between her and Brent, but everyone seemed to have assumed that Brent was the charming hero of the ballroom and that she'd been his desirable date.

"So are you and Brent a hot item now?" Gabe asked in an overly casual tone.

Kat felt a little sick. "Why do you want to know?"

"I don't."

"Gabe, you just asked me."

"So, don't answer if you don't want to tell me. It's not going to change my life."

"Who said it would?!" Kat put her face into her hands, then peered into the audiovisual room.

"Let's go into the station," Gabe finally said, leading her down the hall that was covered with notices and acoustical tile. They cut through the audiovisual room and went into the studio. It smelled dusty. An apple core had been left on the sound-effects box, along with Gabe's old playlist from their last show.

Kat remembered their last show, which had been that previous Friday. The show had been a dud, probably the first time that their routines hadn't quite panned out. Their timing hadn't clicked, and their jokes had fallen flat. But luckily almost everyone had been at a football spirit rally, so most of their audience had been spared.

Kat slipped into Gabe's chair and put her desert boots up on the board.

Gabe leaned back against the music shelf and crossed his arms. He stared at her. "Why do I feel like I haven't seen you for a while?"

"I don't know. You said you saw me at the dance."

"Oh, yeah." He tapped his playlist against his knee and hummed for a while. "So are you and Brent in love?"

Kat pounded the board with her fist. "Why do you keep talking about me and Brent? It's none of your business!"

"I don't keep talking about you and Brent. Why are you so touchy?"

"I'm not touchy. And I don't really want to talk about me and Brent right now. Do you mind?"

"All right." He held up his hands and frowned. "So what do you want to talk about?"

"Why don't we just rehearse for our next show," she decided. That sounded fairly safe.

"Okay." He shrugged. "What's our topic?"

"Anything."

"Anything?"

"That's what I said. Anything."

Gabe huffed.

Kat blurted out. "Just as long as it's nothing to do with guys, sex, dating, love, romance, all of the above, take your choice and don't skip any questions please."

Gabe finally smiled. Then he tousled her hair and started to give her a hug. But when she tensed, he attempted a funny handshake instead.

Kat was startled to feel the sudden pull of tears. Both of them were quiet while the dust settled and the wheels on Gabe's chair squeaked.

Finally Gabe leaned back against the music shelf again. He stretched out his arms and snapped his fingers. "Okay. So, shall we start working on this? I assume you will still want to do our radio show?"

She didn't respond.

"I take it that means yes," he decided. "Am I right?"

She shrugged.

"Gee, don't get too excited." He shook his head. "So we still need a topic. How about chess club, thespians, wrestling team."

Kat took a deep breath. Nothing would come into her brain. "Soccer tryouts, health class, salt-water taffy, auto shop," she babbled, knowing they'd already covered all those.

"Oh, wait, oh. I've got it!" Gabe cried, pounding on the music shelf. "How about the new quad and the new cafeteria, how there's going to be so much noise that nobody will be able to study or concentrate. Our school looks great, but we all flunk out!"

"I like that," Kat had to admit.

"Me, too." Gabe gave her a thumbs up.

Kat finally smiled. "Okay. Let's run with it, partner."

"Okay, buddy," Gabe nodded. His eyes lingered on her, revealing sadness and regret. "Let's travel. . . ."

"Two sure isn't a crowd, is it, Chip?"

"Everybody's just freaked about what happened at the dance," Chip told Jojo at the end of lunch. "I kind of wish I'd gone now, after hearing about what happened."

"No, you don't," Jojo said.

"Huh?"

"You don't wish that you'd gone, Chip. Not if your date had been Lisa."

Chip leaned back against Jojo's locker with a puzzled expression while the two of them watched the work being done on the quad. The loud digging machine was taking a break, and now some carpenters were making a frame to pour a new cement walkway.

"Have you seen Miranda?" Chip asked, sweeping his long hair away from his face and finishing his sandwich.

"Not today."

"I won't ask if Eric is going to keep joining us for lunch," Chip commented. "Somehow I think he's going to go back to his senior friends."

Jojo nodded.

The bell rang, and Chip started stuffing his books back into his backpack. When he'd slung the pack over his shoulder and was ready to leave, he turned back and asked, "So why did you say it was better that I didn't go with Lisa? Did something happen?"

Jojo thought for a moment. She still didn't know what to do with all the juicy info she was keeping inside her head. But once again, she resisted the urge to spit it out. "No. Nothing happened. I've just been thinking about Lisa, that's all."

Chip nodded.

"She just isn't good enough for you," Jojo added, stopping him as he was about to leave for class. "That's all."

"Yeah?" Chip looked like he knew Jojo was laying on the flattery, but that he appreciated it, anyway. "Yeah, well, actually I took out this freshman girl who I know from the Environmentalists on Saturday night. We went bowling and to a movie and we had a pretty terrific time." He waved to Jojo and smiled. "Hey, Jojo. You want a ride home today?" he called back from the hall.

"Okay."

"Good. See you after school."

Jojo waved and then turned back to her locker, content for once to actually be alone. She checked her mirror and sorted through her books, thinking about how football season was over and wondering if they would get new uniforms. She was already fantasizing about the perfect new style of flared skirt with maybe a V-necked sweater this time when she realized that someone was standing next to her.

Leanne.

Jojo made sure she wasn't in Leanne's way. Then she continued sorting through her locker, waiting to be scolded or snubbed. But Leanne did nothing. For once she even opened her locker door without waiting for Jojo to walk away first.

Jojo peeked inside. Leanne's locker was packed to the brim. Jojo saw a box of hair color and some high heels, a hot pot, a furry jacket, and some packages of instant soup. Leanne continued to ignore her, until she'd found the book she'd needed and had managed to force her locker door closed again. Jojo redid her lipstick and closed her locker, too.

But just before Leanne left, she stopped and looked at Jojo. "Hello," Leanne said.

"Hello," Jojo echoed.

That was all. Then Leanne hugged her textbook and joined the flow of students scurrying to class.

At the end of the day, Miranda was standing outside the guidance office, staring at the glass-covered bulletin board. She had her notebook out and her pencil sharpened, but the harder she stared the more it all blurred in front of her. Honor Society. Pep Club. Friends in Need. It was all still there and it was all important, but it didn't fit into the same space inside her brain.

Then she heard footsteps and her heart

stopped. Jackson had left her a note that morning over the Friends in Need flier, asking to meet her there after school. All day she wanted to see him, ached to see him, but at the same time, something inside her was shutting down, closing up from fear. She almost ran away before he found her.

But Jackson quickly appeared, running down from the stairwell, wearing his leather jacket and torn jeans. As soon as he reached her, she took a step back.

"I called you yesterday," Jackson assured her in an urgent tone.

"You did?"

"Of course I did. Your father wouldn't even let me talk to you."

Even though she'd been waiting so long to see Jackson again, Miranda could barely look him in the face. Her entire Sunday had been spent hearing how she'd failed her parents and Eric, how she'd thrown away everything and everyone that had ever mattered. "My father won't let me talk to anyone. I haven't talked to Eric or to any of my friends."

Jackson reached for her, but she stiffened and stepped back again. "Miranda."

"My father won't let me go out, either," she recited. "No after-school meetings. Nothing." She checked her watch. "I have to leave right now. My mom is even picking me up at school to make sure I don't spend time with you."

"Is that it then?" he asked in a stunned voice. "Your parents say you can't see me, and that's the end?"

"What am I supposed to do?"

He stared at her, and she told herself to leave. Her mother was waiting. She knew what she was supposed to do. But as strongly as she wanted to keep her eyes down and walk right by, she couldn't help glancing at Jackson's face just one last time. And that's when it all came flooding back, everything she'd been trying not to think about for the last day and a half.

She ran toward him, dropping her books and throwing herself against his chest. His arms engulfed her, and he held her as if he would never let go. When he finally relaxed his embrace, she took in his green eyes, his funny hair, and sad smile. Then his hands were on her face and they were kissing. No hall kiss this time. They were almost frantic. It was a kiss that brought back every moment of a night on a sandy, moonlit beach.

"What are we going to do? How are we going to see each other?" he pleaded.

"I don't know," Miranda gasped. "We'll just have to find a way." She took one last look, kissed him one last time, then ran quickly down the hall.

Kat McDonough continues to fall under gorgeous Brent Tucker's smooth-talking spell, but now there's another girl in the picture . . . and it's one of her best friends! Will anyone win Brent's undying affection? Is he worth it?

Jealous of Brent and Kat, Gabe Sachs's incessant flirting gets him in way over his head. Now he's stuck in a relationship with a girl he doesn't even want!

Meanwhile, Miranda Jamison and Jackson Magruder are busy falling in love as Eric Geraci plots his revenge. Is the romance doomed before it even gets started?

And what does love have in store for Leanne Heard and Chip Kohler?

Don't miss book #2 in the brand-new series: TOTALLY HOT!

LET GO

HANG ON

TELL HIM "YES"

PLAY HARD TO GET

TELL HIM "LET'S JUST BE FRIENDS"

HAVE A PARTY

TELL HIM "NO"

FIGHT PEER PRESSURE

HANG OUT

PROMISE TO BE FRIENDS FOREVER

ASK YOUR BEST FRIEND WHAT SHE WOULD DO...